COOL
SCHOOL STORIES

RED FOX

A Red Fox Book

Published by Random House Children's Books
20 Vauxhall Bridge Road, London SW1V 2SA

A division of Random House UK Ltd
London Melbourne Sydney Auckland
Johannesburg and agencies throughout the world

3 5 7 9 10 8 6 4 2

The Worst Kids in the World first published in Great Britain by Faber & Faber Ltd 1974, *The Worst Kids in the World Best School Year Ever* first published in Great Britain by Red Fox 1996, *Wasim in the Deep End* first published in Great Britain by Julia MacRae 1997, *Follow that Bus!* firt published in Great Britain by The Bodley Head 1977

Red Fox edition 1998

Printed and bound in Great Britain by
Cox & Wyman Ltd, Reading, Berkshire

Papers used by Random House UK Ltd are natural, recyclable products made from wood grown in sustainable forests. The manufacturing processes conform to the environmental regulations of the country of origin.

Random House UK Limited Reg. No. 954009

ISBN 0 09 926585 0

CONTENTS

THE WORST KIDS IN THE WORLD

Barbara Robinson

CHAPTER ONE

The Herdmans were absolutely the worst kids in the history of the world. They lied and stole and smoked cigars (even the girls) and talked dirty and hit little kids and cussed their teachers and took the name of the Lord in vain and set fire to Fred Shoemaker's old broken-down toolhouse.

The toolhouse burned right down to the ground, and I think that surprised the Herdmans. They set fire to things all the time, but that was the first time they managed to burn down a whole building.

I guess it was an accident. I don't suppose they woke up that morning and said to one another, 'Let's go burn down Fred Shoemaker's toolhouse' . . . but maybe they did. After all, it was a Saturday, and not much going on.

It was a terrific fire – two engines and two police cars and all the volunteer firemen and five dozen doughnuts sent up from the Tasti-Lunch Diner. The doughnuts were supposed to be for the firemen, but by the time they got the fire out the doughnuts were all gone. The Herdmans got them – what they couldn't eat they stuffed in their pockets and down the front of their shirts. You could actually *see* the doughnuts all around Ollie Herdman's middle.

I couldn't understand why the Herdmans were hanging around the scene of their crime. Everybody knew the whole thing was their fault, and you'd think they'd have the brains to get out of sight.

One fireman even collared Claude Herdman and said, 'Did you kids start this fire, smoking cigars in that toolhouse?'

But Claude just said, 'We weren't smoking cigars.'

And they weren't. They were playing with Leroy Herdman's 'Young Einstein' chemistry set, which he stole from the hardware store, and that was how they started the fire.

Leroy said so. 'We mixed all the little powders together,' he said, 'and poured lighter fluid around on them and set fire to the lighter fluid. We wanted to see if the chemistry set was any good.'

Any other kid – even a mean kid – would have been a little bit worried if he stole $4.95 worth of something and then burned down a building with it. But Leroy was just mad because the chemistry set got burned up along with everything else before he had a chance to make one or two bombs.

The fire chief got us all together – there were fifteen or twenty kids standing around watching the fire – and gave us a little talk about playing with matches and gasoline and dangerous things like that.

'I don't say that's what happened here,' he told us. 'I don't *know* what happened here, but that could have been it, and you see the result. So let this be a good lesson to you, boys and girls.'

Of course it was a great lesson to the Herdmans – they learned that wherever there's a fire there will be free doughnuts sooner or later.

I guess things would have been different if they'd burned down, say, the Second Presbyterian Church instead of the toolhouse, but the toolhouse was about to fall down anyway. All the neighbours had pestered Mr. Shoemaker to do something about it because it looked so awful and was sure to bring rats. So everybody said the fire was a blessing in disguise, and even Mr. Shoemaker said it was a relief. My father said it was the only good thing the Herdmans ever did, and if they'd *known* it was a good thing, they wouldn't have done it at all. They would have set fire to something else . . . or somebody.

They were just so all-around awful you could hardly believe they were real: Ralph, Imogene, Leroy, Claude, Ollie, and Gladys – six skinny, stringy-haired kids all alike except for being different sizes and having different black-and-blue places where they had clonked each other.

They lived over a garage at the bottom of Sproul Hill. Nobody used the garage any more, but the Herdmans used to bang the door up and down just as fast as they could and try to squash one another – that was their idea of a game. Where other people had grass in their front yard, the Herdmans had rocks. And where other people had hydrangea bushes, the Herdmans had poison ivy.

There was also a sign in the yard that said 'Beware Of The Cat'.

New kids always laughed about that till they got a look at the cat. It was the meanest looking animal I ever saw. It had one short leg and a broken tail and one missing eye, and the mailman wouldn't deliver anything to the Herdmans because of it.

'I don't think it's a regular cat at all,' the mailman told my father. 'I think those kids went up in the hills and caught themselves a bobcat.'

'Oh, I don't think you can tame a wild bobcat,' my father said.

'I'm sure you can't,' said the mailman. 'They'd never try to *tame* it; they'd just try to make it wilder than it was to begin with.'

If that was their plan, it worked – the cat would attack anything it could see out of its one eye.

One day Claude Herdman emptied the whole first grade in three minutes flat when he took the cat to Show-and-Tell. He didn't feed it for two days so it was already mad, and then he carried it to school in a box, and when he opened the box the cat shot out – right straight up in the air, people said.

It came down on the top blackboard ledge and clawed four big long scratches all the way down the blackboard. Then it just tore around all over the place, scratching little kids and shedding fur and scattering books and papers everywhere.

The teacher, Miss Brandel, yelled for everybody to run out in the hall, and she pulled a coat over her head and grabbed a broom and tried to corner the cat. But of course she couldn't see, with the coat over her head, so she just ran up and down the aisles, hollering 'Here, kitty!' and smacking the broom down whenever the cat hissed back. She knocked over the Happy Family dollhouse and a globe of the world, and broke the aquarium full of twenty gallons of water and about sixty-five goldfish.

All the time she kept yelling for Claude to come and catch his cat, but Claude had gone out in the hall with the rest of the class.

Later, when Miss Brandel was slapping Band-Aids on everyone who could show her any blood, she asked Claude why in the world he didn't come and get his cat under control.

'You told us to go out in the hall,' Claude said, just as if he were the ordinary kind of first-grader who did whatever teachers said to do.

The cat settled down a little bit once it got something to eat – most of the goldfish and Ramona Billian's two pet mice that she brought to Show-and-Tell. Ramona cried and carried on so – 'I can't even bury them!' she said – that they sent her home.

The room was a wreck – broken glass and papers and books and puddles of water and dead goldfish everywhere. Miss Brandel was sort of a wreck too, and most of the first-graders were hysterical, so somebody took them outdoors and let them have recess for the rest of the day.

Claude took the cat home and after that there was a rule that you couldn't bring anything alive to Show-and-Tell.

11

The Herdmans moved from grade to grade through the Woodrow Wilson School like those South American fish that strip your bones clean in three minutes flat . . . which was just about what they did to one teacher after another.

But they never, never got kept back in a grade.

When it came time for Claude Herdman to pass to the second grade he didn't know his ABCs or his numbers or his colours or his shapes or his 'Three Bears' or how to get along with anybody. But Miss Brandel passed him anyway.

For one thing, she knew she'd have Ollie Herdman the next year. That was the thing about the Herdmans – there was always another one coming along, and no teacher was crazy enough to let herself in for two of them at once.

I was always in the same grade with Imogene Herdman, and what I did was stay out of her way. It wasn't easy to stay out of her way. You couldn't do it if you were very pretty or very ugly, or very smart or very dumb, or had anything unusual about you, like red hair or double-jointed thumbs.

But if you were sort of a medium kid like me, and kept your mouth shut when the teacher said, 'Who can name all fifty states?' you had a pretty good chance to stay clear of Imogene.

As far as anyone could tell, Imogene was just like the rest of the Herdmans. She never learned anything either, except dirty words and secrets about everybody.

Twice a year we had to go to the health room

to get weighed and measured, and Imogene always managed to find out exactly what everybody weighed. Sometimes she would hang around waiting for the nurse, Miss Hemphill, to give her a Band-Aid; sometimes she would sneak behind the curtain where they kept a folding cot and just stay there the whole time, with one eye on the scales.

'Why are you still here, Imogene?' Miss Hemphill asked one day. 'You can go back to your room.'

'I think you better look and see if I've got what Ollie has.'

'What does Ollie have?'

Imogene shrugged. 'We don't know. Red spots all over.'

Miss Hemphill looked at her. 'What did the doctor say?'

'We didn't have a doctor.' Imogene began scrunching her back up and down against the medicine cabinet.

'Well, does Ollie have a fever? Is he in bed?'

'No, he's in the first grade.'

'Right now?' Miss Hemphill stared. 'Why, he shouldn't be in school with red spots! It could be measles or chicken pox . . . any number of things . . . contagious things. What are you doing?'

'Scratching my back,' Imogene said. 'Boy, do I itch!'

'The rest of you boys and girls go back to your classroom,' Miss Hemphill said, 'and, Imogene, you stay right here.'

So we all went back to our room, and Miss Hemphill went to the first grade to look at Ollie, and Imogene stayed in the health room and copied down everybody's weight from Miss Hemphill's records.

Your weight was supposed to be a big secret, like what you got on your report card.

'It's nobody's business what you get on your report card,' all the teachers said. And Miss Hemphill said the same thing – 'It's nobody's business what you weigh.'

Not even the fat kids could find out what they weighed but Imogene always knew.

'Don't let Albert Pelfrey on the swing,' she would yell at recess. 'He'll bust it. Albert Pelfrey weighs a hundred and forty-three pounds. Last time he weighed a hundred and thirty-seven.' So right away everybody knew two things about Albert – we knew exactly how fat he was, and we also knew that he was getting fatter all the time.

'You have to go to fat-camp this summer,' Imogene hollered at him. 'Miss Hemphill wrote it down on your paper.'

Fat-camp is a place where they feed you lettuce and grapefruit and cottage cheese and eggs for a month, and you either give up and cheat or give up and get skinny.

'I am not!' Albert said. 'I'm going to Disneyland with my Uncle Frank.'

'That's what you think!' Imogene told him.

Albert had to believe her – she was always right about things like that – so all year he had fat-camp to look forward to instead of Disneyland.

Sometimes Imogene would blackmail the fat kids if they had anything she wanted . . . like Wanda Pierce's charm bracelet.

Wanda Pierce weighed about a ton – she even had fat eyes – and her hobby was this charm bracelet. It had twenty-two charms and every single one did something: the little wheels turned, or the little bitty piano keys went 'plink', or the little tiny drawers opened and closed.

Besides being a fat kid, Wanda was also a rich kid, so every time you turned around she had a new charm.

'Look at my new charm,' she would say. 'It cost $6.95 without the tax. It's a bird, and when you push this little knob, its wings flutter. It cost $6.95.'

They were great charms, but everybody got sick of hearing about them, so it was almost a relief when Imogene blackmailed her out of it.

'I know how much you weigh, Wanda,' Imogene told her. 'I wrote it down on this piece of paper. See?'

It must have been an awful amount, because even Wanda looked horrified. So Imogene got her charm bracelet, and she got Lucille Golden's imitation alligator pocketbook with 'Souvenir of Florida' written on it. For a while she got ten cents a week from Floyd Brush, till Floyd caught double pneumonia and lost fifteen pounds and didn't care anymore.

My friend Alice Wendleken was so nasty-clean that she had detergent hands by the time she was four years old. Just the same, Alice picked up a case of head lice when she was at summer camp, and somehow Imogene found out about that. She would sneak up on Alice at recess and holler 'Cooties!' and smack Alice's head. She nearly knocked Alice cross-eyed before one of the teachers saw her and took both of them in to the principal.

'Now, what's this all about?' the principal wanted to know, but Alice wouldn't say.

'I *had* to hit her,' Imogene told him. 'She's got cooties, and I saw one crawling in her hair, and I don't want them on me.'

'You did not see one!' Alice said. 'I don't have them any more!'

'What do you mean, you don't have them anymore?' the principal said. 'Did you have them *lately*?' It really shook him up – he didn't want a whole school full of kids with cooties. So he sent Alice to the health room and the nurse went all through her head with a fine-tooth comb and a magnifying glass, and finally said it was all right.

But it was too late – everybody called Alice 'Cooties' the whole rest of the year.

If Imogene didn't know a secret about a person, she would make one up. She would catch you in the girls' room or out in the hall and whisper, 'I know what you did!' and then you'd go crazy trying to figure out what it was you did that Imogene knew about.

It was no good trying to get secrets on the Herdmans. Everybody already knew about the awful things they did. You couldn't even tease them about their parents, or holler 'Your father's in jail!' because they didn't care. Actually, they didn't know what their father was or where he was or anything about him, because when Gladys was two years old he climbed on a railroad train and disappeared. Nobody blamed him.

Now and then you'd see Mrs. Herdman, walking the cat on a length of chain around the block. But she worked double shifts at the shoe factory, and wasn't home much.

My mother's friend, Miss Philips, was a social-service worker and she tried to get some welfare money for the Herdmans, so Mrs. Herdman could just work one shift and spend more time with her children. But Mrs. Herdman wouldn't do it; she liked the work, she said.

'It's not the work,' Miss Philips told my mother, 'and it's not the money. It's just that she'd rather be at the shoe factory than shut up at home with that crowd of kids.' She sighed. 'I can't say I blame her.'

So the Herdmans pretty much looked after themselves. Ralph looked after Imogene, and Imogene looked after Leroy, and Leroy looked after Claude and so on down the line. The Herdmans were like most big families – the big ones taught the little ones everything they knew . . . and the proof of that was that the meanest Herdman of all was Gladys, the youngest.

We figured they were headed straight for hell, by way of the state penitentiary . . . until they got themselves mixed up with the church, and my mother, and our Christmas pageant.

CHAPTER TWO

Mother didn't expect to have anything to do with the Christmas pageant except to make me and my little brother Charlie be in it (we didn't want to) and to make my father go and see it (he didn't want to).

Every year he said the same thing – 'I've seen the Christmas pageant.'

'You haven't seen this year's Christmas pageant,' Mother would tell him. 'Charlie is a shepherd this year.'

'Charlie was a shepherd last year. No . . . you go on and go. I'm just going to put on my bathrobe and sit by the fire and relax. There's never anything different about the Christmas pageant.'

'There's something different this year,' Mother said.

'What?'

'Charlie is wearing your bathrobe.'

So that year my father went . . . to see his bathrobe, he said.

Actually, he went every year but it was always a struggle, and Mother said that was her contribution to the Christmas pageant – getting my father to go to it.

But then she got stuck with the whole thing when Mrs. George Armstrong fell and broke her leg.

We knew about this as soon as it happened, because Mrs. Armstrong only lived a block and a half away. We heard the siren and saw the ambulance and watched the policemen carry her out of the house on a stretcher.

'Call Mr. Armstrong at his work!' she yelled at the policemen. 'Shut off the stove under my potatoes! Inform the Ladies' Aid that I won't be at the meeting!'

One of the neighbour women called out, 'Helen, are you in much pain?' and Mrs. Armstrong yelled back, 'Yes, terrible! Don't let those children tear up my privet hedge!'

Even in pain, Mrs. Armstrong could still give orders. She was so good at giving orders that she was just naturally the head of anything she belonged to, and at church she did everything but preach. Most of all, she ran the Christmas pageant every year. And here she was, two weeks before Thanksgiving, flat on her back.

'I don't know what they'll do now about the pageant,' Mother said.

But the pageant wasn't the only problem. Mrs. Armstrong was also chairman of the Ladies' Aid Bazaar, and co-ordinator of the Women's Society Pot-luck Supper, and there was a lot of telephoning back and forth to see who would take over those jobs.

Mother had a list of names, and while she was

calling people about the Ladies' Aid Bazaar, Mrs. Homer McCarthy was trying to call Mother about the pot-luck supper. But Mrs. McCarthy got somebody else to do that, and Mother got somebody else to do the bazaar. So the only thing left was the Christmas pageant.

And Mother got stuck with that.

'I could run the pot-luck supper with one hand tied behind my back,' Mother told us. 'All you have to do is make sure everybody doesn't bring meat loaf. But the Christmas pageant!'

Our Christmas pageant isn't what you'd call four-star entertainment. Mrs. Armstrong breaking her leg was the only unexpected thing that ever happened to it. The script is standard (the inn, the stable, the shepherds, the star), and so are the costumes, and so is the casting.

Primary kids are angels; intermediate kids are shepherds; big boys are Wise Men; Elmer Hopkins, the minister's son, has been Joseph for as long as I can remember; and my friend Alice Wendleken is Mary because she's so smart, so neat and clean, and, most of all, so holy-looking.

All the rest of us are the angel choir – lined up according to height because nobody can sing parts. As a matter of fact, nobody can *sing*. We're strictly a no-talent outfit except for a girl named Alberta Bottles, who whistles. Last year Alberta whistled 'What Child Is This?' for a change of pace, but nobody liked it, especially Mrs. Bottles, because Alberta put too much into it and ran out of air and

21

passed out cold on the manger in the middle of the third verse.

Aside from that, though, it's always just the Christmas story, year after year, with people shuffling around in bathrobes and bedsheets and sharp wings.

'Well,' my father said, once Mother got put in charge of it, 'here's your big chance. Why don't you cancel the pageant and show movies?'

'Movies of what?' Mother said.

'I don't know. Fred Stamper has five big reels of Yellowstone National Park.'

'What does Yellowstone National Park have to do with Christmas?' Mother asked.

'I know a good movie,' Charlie said. 'We had it at school. It shows a heart operation, and two kids got sick.'

'Never mind,' Mother said. 'I guess you all think you're pretty funny, but the Christmas pageant is a tradition, and I don't plan to do anything different.'

Of course nobody even thought about the Herdmans in connection with the Christmas pageant. Most of us spent all week in school being pounded and poked and pushed around by Herdmans, and we looked forward to Sunday as a real day of rest.

Once a month the whole Sunday School would go to church for the first fifteen minutes of the service and do something special – sing a song, or act out a parable, or recite Bible verses. Usually the little kids sang 'Jesus Loves Me,' which was all they were up to.

But when my brother Charlie was in with the little

kids, his teacher thought up something different to do. She had everybody write down on a piece of paper what they liked best about Sunday school, or draw a picture of what they liked best. And when we all got in the church she stood up in front of the congregation and said, 'Today some of our youngest boys and girls are going to tell you what Sunday school means to them. Betsy, what do you have on your paper?'

Betsy Cathcart stood up and said, 'What I like best about Sunday school is the good feeling I get when I go there.'

I don't think she wrote that down at all, but it sounded terrific, of course.

One kid said he liked hearing all the Bible stories. Another kid said, 'I like learning songs about Jesus.'

Eight or nine little kids stood up and said what they liked, and it was always something good about Jesus or God or cheerful friends or the nice teacher.

Finally the teacher said, 'I think we have time for one more. Charlie, what can you tell us about Sunday school?'

My little brother Charlie stood up and he didn't even have to look at his piece of paper. 'What I like best about Sunday school,' he said, 'is that there aren't any Herdmans here.'

Well. The teacher should have stuck with 'Jesus Loves Me', because everybody forgot all the nice churchy things the other kids said, and just remembered what Charlie said about the Herdmans.

When we went to pick him up after church his

teacher told us, 'I'm sure there are many things that Charlie likes about Sunday school. Maybe he will tell you what some of them are.' She smiled at all of us, but you could tell she was really mad.

On the way home I asked Charlie, 'What are some of the other things you like that she was talking about?'

He shrugged. 'I like all the other stuff but she said to write down what we liked best, and what I like best is no Herdmans.'

'Not a very Christian sentiment,' my father said.

'Maybe not, but it's a very practical one,' Mother told him – last year Charlie had spent the whole second grade being black-and-blue because he had to sit next to Leroy Herdman.

In the end it was Charlie's fault that the Herdmans showed up in church.

For three days in a row Leroy Herdman stole the dessert from Charlie's lunch box and finally Charlie just gave up trying to do anything about it. 'Oh, go on and take it,' he said. 'I don't care. I get all the dessert I want in Sunday school.'

Leroy wanted to know more about that. 'What kind of dessert?' he said.

'Chocolate cake,' Charlie told him, 'and candy bars and cookies and Kool-Aid. We get refreshments all the time, all we want.'

'You're a liar,' Leroy said.

Leroy was right. We got jelly beans at Easter and punch and cookies on Children's Day, and that was it.

'We get ice cream, too,' Charlie went on, 'and doughnuts and popcorn balls.'

'Who gives it to you?' Leroy wanted to know.

'The minister,' Charlie said. He didn't know who else to say.

Of course that was the wrong thing to tell Herdmans if you wanted them to stay away. And sure enough, the very next Sunday there they were, slouching into Sunday school, eyes peeled for the refreshments.

'Where do you get the cake?' Ralph asked the Sunday school superintendent, and Mr. Grady said, 'Well, son, I don't know about any cake, but they're collecting the food packages out in the kitchen.' What he meant was the canned stuff we brought in every year as a Thanksgiving present for the Orphans Home.

It was just our bad luck that the Herdmans picked that Sunday to come, because when they saw all the cans of spaghetti and beans and grape drink and peanut butter, they figured there might be some truth to what Charlie said about refreshments.

So they stayed. They didn't sing any hymns or say any prayers, but they did make a little money, because I saw Imogene snake a handful of coins out of the collection basket when it went past her.

At the end of the morning Mr. Grady came to every class and made an announcement.

'We'll be starting rehearsals soon for our Christmas pageant,' he said, 'and next week after the service we'll all gather in the back of the church to decide who will play the main roles. But of course we want every boy and girl in our Sunday school to take part in the pageant, so be sure your parents know that you'll be staying a little later next Sunday.'

Mr. Grady made this same speech every year, so he didn't get any wild applause. Besides, as I said, we all knew what part we were going to play anyway.

Alice Wendleken must have been a little bit worried, though, because she turned around to me with this sticky smile on her face and said, 'I hope you're going to be in the angel choir again. You're so good in the angel choir.'

What she meant was, I hope you won't get to be Mary just because your mother's running the pageant. She didn't have to worry. I didn't want to be Mary. I didn't want to be in the angel choir either, but everybody had to be something.

All of a sudden Imogene Herdman dug me in the ribs with her elbow. She has the sharpest elbows of anybody I ever knew. 'What's the pageant?' she said.

'It's a play,' I said, and for the first time that day (except when she saw the collection basket) Imogene looked interested. All the Herdmans are big movie-goers, though they never pay their own way. One or two of them start a fight at the box office of the theatre while the others slip in. They get their popcorn the same way, and then they spread out all over the place so the manager can never find them all before the picture's over.

'What's the play about?' Imogene asked.

'It's about Jesus,' I said.

'Everything here is,' she muttered, so I figured Imogene didn't care much about the Christmas pageant.

But I was wrong.

CHAPTER THREE

Mrs. Armstrong, who was still trying to run things from her hospital bed, said that the same people always got the main parts. 'But it's important to give everybody a chance,' she told Mother over the telephone. 'Let me tell you what I do.'

Mother sighed, and turned off the heat under the pork chops. 'All right, Helen,' she said.

Mrs. Armstrong called Mother at least every other day, and she always called at suppertime. 'Don't let me interrupt your supper,' she always said, and then went right ahead and did it anyway, while my father paced up and down the hall, saying things under his breath about Mrs. Armstrong.

'Here's what I do,' Mrs. Armstrong said. 'I get them all together and tell them about the rehearsals, and that they must be on time and pay close attention. Then I tell them that the main parts are Mary and Joseph and the Wise Men and the Angel of the Lord. And then I always remind them that there are no small parts, only small actors.'

'Do they understand what that means?' Mother asked.

'Oh, yes,' Mrs. Armstrong said.

Later Mother asked me if I knew what that meant, about small parts and small actors.

I didn't really know – none of us did. It was just something Mrs. Armstrong always said. 'I guess it means that the short kids have to be in the front row of the angel choir, or else nobody can see them.'

'I thought so,' Mother said. 'It doesn't mean that at all. It really means that every single person in the pageant is just as important as every other person – that the littlest baby angel is just as important as Mary.'

'Go and tell that to Alice Wendleken,' I said, and Mother told me not to be so fresh. She didn't get very mad, though, because she knew I was right. You could have a Christmas pageant without *any* baby angels, but you couldn't have one without a Mary.

Mrs. Armstrong knew it too. 'I always start with Mary,' she told Mother over the telephone. 'I tell them that we must choose our Mary carefully, because Mary was the mother of Jesus.'

'I know that,' Mother said, wanting to get off the telephone and cook the pork chops.

'Yes. I tell them that our Mary should be a cheerful, happy little girl who is unselfish and kind to others. Then I tell them about Joseph, that he was God's choice to be Jesus' father, and our Joseph ought to be a little boy . . .' She went on and on and got as far as the second Wise Man when Mother said, 'Helen, I'll have to go now. There's somebody at the door.'

Actually there was somebody at the door. It was

my father, standing out on the porch in his coat and hat, leaning on the doorbell.

When Mother let him in he took off his hat and bowed to her. 'Lady, can you give me some supper? I haven't had a square meal in three days.'

'Oh, for goodness sake,' Mother said, 'Come on in. What will the neighbours think, to see you standing out there ringing your own doorbell? And why didn't you ring the doorbell ten minutes ago?'

Mrs. Armstrong called Mother two more times that week – to tell her that people could hem up costumes, but couldn't cut them – and to tell her not to let the angel choir wear lipstick. And by Sunday, Mother was already sick of the whole thing.

After church we all filed into the back seven pews, along with two or three Sunday-school teachers who were supposed to keep everybody quiet. It was a terrible time to try to keep everybody quiet – all the little kids were tired and all the big kids were hungry, and all the mothers wanted to go home and cook dinner, and all the fathers wanted to go home and watch the football game on TV.

'Now, this isn't going to take very long,' Mother told us. My father had said it better not take very long, because he wanted to watch the football game too. He also wanted to eat, he said – he hadn't had a decent meal all week.

'First I'm going to tell you about the rehearsals,' Mother said. 'We'll have our rehearsals on Wednesdays at 6.30. We're only going to have five rehearsals so you must all try to be present at every one.'

'What if we get sick?' asked a little kid in the front pew.

'You won't get sick,' Mother told him, which was exactly what she told Charlie that morning when Charlie said he didn't want to be a shepherd and would be sick to his stomach if she made him be one.

'Now you little children in the cradle room and the primary class will be our angels,' Mother said. 'You'll like that, won't you?'

They all said yes. What else could they say?

'The older boys and girls will be shepherds and guests at the inn and members of the choir.' Mother was really zipping along, and I thought how mad Mrs. Armstrong would be about all the things she was leaving out.

'And we need Mary and Joseph, the three Wise Men, and the Angel of the Lord. They aren't hard parts, but they're very important parts, so those people must absolutely come to every rehearsal.'

'What if *they* get sick?' It was the same little kid, and it made you wonder what kind of little kid he was, to be so interested in sickness.

'They won't get sick either,' Mother said, looking a little cross. 'Now, we all know what kind of person Mary was. She was quiet and gentle and kind, and the little girl who plays Mary should try to be that kind of person. I know that many of you would like to be Mary in our pageant, but of course we can only have one Mary. So I'll ask for volunteers, and then we'll all decide together which girl should get the part.' That was pretty safe to say, since the only person who ever raised her hand was Alice Wendleken.

But Alice just sat there, chewing on a piece of her hair and looking down at the floor . . . and the only person who raised her hand this time was Imogene Herdman.

'Did you have a question, Imogene?' Mother asked. I guess that was the only reason she could think of for Imogene to have her hand up.

'No,' Imogene said. 'I want to be Mary.' She looked back over her shoulder. 'And Ralph wants to be Joseph.'

'Yeh,' Ralph said.

Mother just stared at them. It was like a detective movie, when the nice little old grey-haired lady sticks a gun in the bank window and says 'Give me all your money' and you can't believe it. Mother couldn't believe this.

'Well,' she said after a minute, 'we want to be sure that everyone has a chance. Does anyone else want to volunteer for Joseph?'

No one did. No one ever did, especially not Elmer Hopkins. But he couldn't do anything about it, because he was the minister's son. One year he didn't volunteer to be Joseph and neither did anyone else, and afterward I heard Reverend Hopkins talking to Elmer out in the hall.

'You're going to be Joseph,' Reverend Hopkins said. 'That's it.'

'I don't want to be Joseph,' Elmer told him. 'I'm too big, and I feel dumb up there, and all those little kids give me a pain in the neck.'

'I can understand that,' Reverend Hopkins said. 'I can even sympathise, but till somebody else volunteers for Joseph, you're stuck with it.'

'Nobody's ever going to do that!' Elmer said. 'I even offered Grady Baker fifty cents to be Joseph and he wouldn't do it. I'm going to have to be Joseph for the rest of my life!'

'Cheer up,' Reverend Hopkins told him. 'Maybe somebody will turn up.'

I'll bet he didn't think the somebody would be Ralph Herdman.

'All right,' Mother said, 'Ralph will be our Joseph. Now, does anyone else want to volunteer for Mary?' Mother looked all around, trying to catch somebody's eye – *anybody's* eye. 'Janet? . . . Roberta? . . . Alice, don't you want to volunteer this year?'

'No,' Alice said, so low you could hardly hear her. 'I don't want to.'

Nobody volunteered to be Wise Men either, except Leroy, Claude, and Ollie Herdman.

So there was my mother, stuck with a Christmas pageant full of Herdmans in the main roles.

There was one Herdman left over, and one main role left over, and you didn't have to be very smart to figure out that Gladys was going to be the Angel of the Lord.

'What do I have to do?' Gladys wanted to know.

33

'The Angel of the Lord was the one who brought the good news to the shepherds,' Mother said.

Right away all the shepherds began to wiggle around in their seats, figuring that any good news Gladys brought them would come with a smack in the teeth.

Charlie's friend Hobie Carmichael raised his hand and said, 'I can't be a shepherd. We're going to Philadelphia.'

'Why didn't you say so before?' Mother asked.

'I forgot.'

Another kid said, 'My mother doesn't want me to be a shepherd.'

'Why not?' Mother said.

'I don't know. She just said don't be a shepherd.'

One kid was honest. 'Gladys Herdman hits too hard,' he said.

'Why, Gladys isn't going to hit anybody!' Mother said. 'What an idea! The Angel just visits the shepherds in the fields and tells them Jesus is born.'

'And hits 'em,' said the kid.

Of course he was right. You could just picture Gladys whamming shepherds left and right, but Mother said that was perfectly ridiculous.

'I don't want to hear another word about it,' she said. 'No shepherds may quit – or get sick,' she added, before the kid in the front pew could ask.

While everybody was leaving, Mother grabbed Alice Wendleken by the arm and said, 'Alice, why in the world didn't you raise your hand to be Mary?'

'I don't know,' Alice said, looking mad.

But I knew – I'd heard Imogene Herdman telling Alice what would happen to her if she dared to volunteer: all the ordinary, everyday Herdman-things like clonking you on the head, and drawing pictures all over your homework papers, and putting worms in your coat pocket.

'I don't care,' Alice told her. 'I don't care what you do. I'm always Mary in the pageant.'

'And next spring,' Imogene went on, squinching up her eyes, 'when the pussy willows come out, I'll stick a pussy willow so far down your ear that nobody can reach it – and it'll sprout there, and it'll grow and grow, and you'll spend the rest of your life with a pussy-willow bush growing out your ear.'

You had to admire her – that was the worst thing any of them ever thought up to do. Of course some people might not think that could happen, but it could. Ollie Herdman did it once. He got this terrible earache in school, and when the nurse looked down his ear with her little lighted tube she yelled so loud you could hear her all the way down the hall. 'He's got something growing down there!' she hollered.

They had to take Ollie to the hospital and put him under and dig this sprouted pussy willow out of his ear.

So that was why Alice kept her mouth shut about being Mary.

'You know she wouldn't do all those things she said,' I told Alice as we walked home.

'Yes, she would,' Alice said. 'Herdmans will do

anything. But your mother should have told them no. Somebody should put Imogene out of the pageant, and all the rest of them too. They'll do something terrible and ruin the whole thing.'

I thought she was probably right, and so did lots of other people, and for two or three days all anybody could talk about was the Herdmans being Mary and Joseph and all.

Mrs. Homer McCarthy called Mother to say that she had been thinking and thinking about it, and if the Herdmans wanted to participate in our Christmas celebration, why didn't we let them hand out programmes at the door?

'We don't have programmes for the Christmas pageant,' Mother said.

'Well, maybe we ought to get some printed and put the Herdmans in charge of that.'

Alice's mother told the Ladies' Aid that it was sacrilegious to let Imogene Herdman be Mary. Somebody we never heard of called up Mother on the telephone and said her name was Hazelbeck and she lived on Sproul Hill, and was it true that Imogene Herdman was going to be Mary the mother of Jesus in a church play?

'Yes,' Mother said. 'Imogene is going to be Mary in our Christmas pageant.'

'And the rest of them too?' the lady asked.

'Yes, Ralph is going to be Joseph and the others are the Wise Men and the Angel of the Lord.'

'You must be crazy,' this Mrs. Hazelbeck told Mother. 'I live next door to that outfit with their yelling and screaming and their insane cat and their garage door going up and down, up and down all day long, and let me tell you, you're in for a rowdy time!'

Some people said it wasn't fair for a whole family who didn't even go to our church to barge in and take over the pageant. My father said somebody better lock up the Women's Society silver service. My mother just said she would rather be in the hospital with Mrs. Armstrong.

But then the flower committee took a potted geranium to Mrs. Armstrong and told her what was going on and she nearly fell out of bed, traction bars and all. 'I feel personally responsible,' she said. 'Whatever happens, I accept the blame. If I'd been up and around and doing my duty, this never would have happened.'

And that made my mother so mad she couldn't see straight.

'If she'd been up and around it wouldn't have happened!' Mother said. 'That woman! She must be surprised that the sun is still coming up every morning without her to supervise the sunrise. Well, let me tell you – '

'Don't tell me,' my father said. 'I'm on your side.'

'I just mean that Helen Armstrong is not the only woman alive who can run a Christmas pageant. Up till now I'd made up my mind just to do the best I could under the circumstances, but *now* – ' She stabbed a meat fork into the pot roast. 'I'm going to make this the very best Christmas pageant anybody ever saw, and I'm going to do it with Herdmans, too.

After all, they raised their hands and nobody else did. And that's that.'

And it was too. For one thing, nobody else wanted to take over the pageant, with or without Herdmans; and for another thing, Reverend Hopkins got fed up with all the complaints and told everybody where to get off.

Of course, he didn't say 'Go jump in the lake, Mrs. Wendleken' or anything like that. He just reminded everyone that when Jesus said 'Suffer the little children to come unto me' Jesus meant all the little children, including Herdmans.

So that shut everybody up, even Alice's mother, and the next Wednesday we started rehearsals.

CHAPTER FOUR

The first pageant rehearsal was usually about as much fun as a three-hour ride on the school bus, and just as noisy and crowded. This rehearsal, though, was different. Everybody shut up and settled down right away, for fear of missing something awful that the Herdmans might do.

They got there ten minutes late, sliding into the room like a bunch of outlaws about to shoot up a saloon. When Leroy passed Charlie he knuckled him behind the ear, and one little primary girl yelled as Gladys went by. But Mother had said she was going to ignore everything except blood, and since the primary kid wasn't bleeding, and neither was Charlie, nothing happened.

Mother said, 'And here's the Herdman family. We're glad to see you all,' which was probably the biggest lie ever said right out loud in the church.

Imogene smiled – the Herdman smile, we called it, sly and sneaky – and there they sat, the closest thing to criminals that we knew about, and they were going to represent the best and most beautiful. No wonder everybody was so worked up.

Mother started to separate everyone into angels

and shepherds and guests at the inn, but right away she ran into trouble.

'Who were the shepherds?' Leroy Herdman wanted to know. 'Where did they come from?'

Ollie Herdman didn't even know what a shepherd was . . . or, anyway, that's what he said.

'What was the inn?' Claude asked. 'What's an inn?'

'It's like a motel,' somebody told him, 'where people go to spend the night.'

'What people?' Claude said. 'Jesus?'

'Oh, honestly!' Alice Wendleken grumbled. 'Jesus wasn't even born yet! Mary and Joseph went there.'

'Why?' Ralph asked.

'What happened first?' Imogene hollered at my mother. 'Begin at the beginning!'

That really scared me because the beginning would be the Book of Genesis, where it says 'In the beginning . . .' and if we were going to have to start with the Book of Genesis we'd never get through.

The thing was, the Herdmans didn't know anything about the Christmas story. They knew that Christmas was Jesus' birthday, but everything else was news to them – the shepherds, the Wise Men, the star, the stable, the crowded inn.

It was hard to believe. At least, it was hard for me to believe – Alice Wendleken said she didn't have any trouble believing it. 'How would they find out about the Christmas story?' she said. 'They don't even know what a Bible is. Look what Gladys did to that Bible last week!'

While Imogene was snitching money from the collection plate in my class, Gladys and Ollie drew moustaches and tails on all the disciples in the primary-grade Illustrated Bible.

'They never went to church in their whole life till your little brother told them we got refreshments,' Alice said, 'and all you ever hear about Christmas in school is how to make ornaments out of aluminium foil. So how would they know about the Christmas story?'

She was right. Of course they might have read about it, but they never read anything except 'Amazing Comics'. And they might have heard about it on TV, except that Ralph paid sixty-five cents for their TV at a garage sale, and you couldn't see anything on it unless somebody held on to the antenna. Even then, you couldn't see much.

The only other way for them to hear about the Christmas story was from their parents, and I guess Mr. Herdman never got around to it before he climbed on the railroad train. And it was pretty clear that Mrs. Herdman had given up ever trying to tell them anything.

So they just didn't know. And Mother said she had better begin by reading the Christmas story from the Bible. This was a pain in the neck to most of us because we knew the whole thing backward and forward and never had to be told anything except who we were supposed to be, and where we were supposed to stand.

' . . . Joseph and Mary, his espoused wife, being great with child . . .'

'Pregnant!' yelled Ralph Herdman.

Well. That stirred things up. All the big kids began to giggle and all the little kids wanted to know what was so funny, and Mother had to hammer on the floor with a blackboard pointer. 'That's enough, Ralph,' she said, and went on with the story.

'I don't think it's very nice to say Mary was pregnant,' Alice whispered to me.

'But she was,' I pointed out. In a way, though, I agreed with her. It sounded too ordinary. Anybody could be pregnant. 'Great with child' sounded better for Mary.

'I'm not supposed to talk about people being pregnant.' Alice folded her hands in her lap and pinched her lips together. 'I'd better tell my mother.'

'Tell her what?'

'That your mother is talking about things like that in church. My mother might not want me to be here.'

I was pretty sure she would do it. She wanted to be Mary, and she was mad at Mother. I knew, too, that she would make it sound worse than it was and Mrs. Wendleken would get madder than she already was. Mrs. Wendleken didn't even want cats to have kittens or birds to lay eggs, and she wouldn't let Alice play with anybody who had two rabbits.

But there wasn't much I could do about it, except pinch Alice, which I did. She yelped, and Mother separated us and made me sit beside Imogene

Herdman and sent Alice to sit in the middle of the baby angels.

I wasn't crazy to sit next to Imogene – after all, I'd spent my whole life staying away from Imogene – but she didn't even notice me . . . not much, anyway.

'Shut up,' was all she said. 'I want to hear her.'

I couldn't believe it. Among other things, the Herdmans were famous for never sitting still and never paying attention to anyone – teachers, parents (their own or anybody else's), the truant officer, the police – yet here they were, eyes glued on my mother and taking in every word.

'What's that?' they would yell whenever they didn't understand the language, and when Mother read about there being no room at the inn, Imogene's jaw dropped and she sat up in her seat.

'My God!' she said. 'Not even for Jesus?'

I saw Alice purse her lips together so I knew that was something else Mrs. Wendleken would hear about – swearing in the church.

'Well, now, after all,' Mother explained, 'nobody knew the baby was going to turn out to be Jesus.'

'You said Mary knew,' Ralph said. 'Why didn't she tell them?'

'*I* would have told them!' Imogene put in. 'Boy, would I have told them! What was the matter with Joseph that he didn't tell them? Her pregnant and everything,' she grumbled.

'What was that they laid the baby in?' Leroy said. 'That manger . . . is that like a bed? Why would they have a bed in the barn?'

'That's just the point,' Mother said. 'They *didn't* have a bed in the barn, so Mary and Joseph had to use whatever there was. What would you do if you had a new baby and no bed to put the baby in?'

'We put Gladys in a bureau drawer,' Imogene volunteered.

'Well, there you are,' Mother said, blinking a little. 'You didn't have a bed for Gladys so you had to use something else.'

'Oh, we had a bed,' Ralph said, 'only Ollie was still in it and he wouldn't get out. He didn't like Gladys.' He elbowed Ollie. 'Remember how you didn't like Gladys?'

I thought that was pretty smart of Ollie, not to like Gladys right off the bat.

'*Anyway*,' Mother said, 'Mary and Joseph used the manger. A manger is a large wooden feeding trough for animals.'

'What were the wadded-up clothes?' Claude wanted to know.

'The what?' Mother said.

'You read about it – "she wrapped him in wadded-up clothes".'

'*Swaddling* clothes.' Mother sighed. 'Long ago, people used to wrap their babies very tightly in big pieces of material, so they couldn't move around. It made the babies feel cosy and comfortable.'

I thought it probably just made the babies mad. Till then, I didn't know what swaddling clothes were either, and they sounded terrible, so I wasn't too surprised when Imogene got all excited about that.

'You mean they tied him up and put him in a feedbox?' she said. 'Where was the Child Welfare?'

The Child Welfare was always checking up on the Herdmans. I'll bet if the Child Welfare had ever found Gladys all tied up in a bureau drawer they would have done something about it.

'And, lo, the Angel of the Lord came upon them,' Mother went on, 'and the glory of the Lord shone round about them, and – '

'Shazam!' Gladys yelled, flinging her arms out and smacking the kid next to her.

'What?' Mother said. Mother never read 'Amazing Comics'.

'Out of the black night with horrible vengeance, the Mighty Marvo – '

'I don't know what you're talking about, Gladys,' Mother said. 'This is the Angel of the Lord who comes to the shepherds in the fields, and – '

'Out of nowhere, right?' Gladys said. 'In the black night, right?'

'Well . . .' Mother looked unhappy. 'In a way.'

So Gladys sat back down, looking very satisfied, as if this was at least one part of the Christmas story that made sense to her.

'Now when Jesus was born in Bethlehem of Judaea,' Mother went on reading, 'behold there came Wise Men from the East to Jerusalem, saying – '

'That's you, Leroy,' Ralph said, 'and Claude and Ollie. So pay attention.'

'What does it mean, Wise Men?' Ollie wanted to know. 'Were they like schoolteachers?'

'No, dumbbell,' Claude said. 'It means like President of the United States.'

Mother looked surprised, and a little pleased – like she did when Charlie finally learned the times-tables up to five. 'Why, that's very close, Claude,' she said. 'Actually, they were kings.'

'Well, it's about time,' Imogene muttered. 'Maybe they'll tell the innkeeper where to get off, and get the baby out of the barn.'

'They saw the young child with Mary, his mother, and fell down and worshipped him, and presented unto him gifts: gold, and frankincense, and myrrh.'

'What's that stuff?' Leroy wanted to know.

'Precious oils,' Mother said, 'and fragrant resins.'

'Oil!' Imogene hollered. 'What kind of a cheap king hands out oil for a present? You get better presents from the firemen!'

Sometimes the Herdmans got Christmas presents at the Firemen's Party, but the Santa Claus always had to feel all around the packages to be sure they weren't getting bows and arrows or dart guns or anything like that. Imogene usually got sewing cards or jigsaw puzzles and she never liked them, but I guess she figured they were better than oil.

Then we came to King Herod, and the Herdmans never heard of him either, so Mother had to explain that it was Herod who sent the Wise Men to find the baby Jesus.

'Was it him that sent the crummy presents?' Ollie wanted to know, and Mother said it was worse than that – he planned to have the baby Jesus put to death.

'My God!' Imogene said. 'He just got born and already they're out to kill him!'

The Herdmans wanted to know all about Herod – what he looked like, and how rich he was, and whether he fought wars with people.

'He must have been the main king,' Claude said, 'if he could make the other three do what he wanted them to.'

'If I was a king,' Leroy said, 'I wouldn't let some other king push me around.'

'You couldn't help it if he was the main king.'

'I'd go be king somewhere else.'

They were really interested in Herod, and I figured they liked him. He was so mean he could have been their ancestor – Herod Herdman. But I was wrong.

'Who's going to be Herod in this play?' Leroy said.

'We don't show Herod in our pageant,' Mother said. And they all got mad. They wanted somebody to be Herod so they could beat up on him.

I couldn't understand the Herdmans. You would have thought the Christmas story came right out of the F.B.I. files, they got so involved in it – wanted a bloody end to Herod, worried about Mary having her baby in a barn, and called the Wise Men a bunch of dirty spies.

And they left the first rehearsal arguing about whether Joseph should have set fire to the inn, or just chased the innkeeper into the next county.

CHAPTER FIVE

When we got home my father wanted to hear all about it.

'Well,' Mother said, 'just suppose you had never heard the Christmas story, and didn't know anything about it, and then somebody told it to you. What would you think?'

My father looked at her for a minute or two and then he said, 'Well, I guess I would think it was pretty disgraceful that they couldn't find any room for a pregnant woman except in the stable.'

I was amazed. It didn't seem natural for my father to be on the same side as the Herdmans. But then, it didn't seem natural for the Herdmans to be on the *right* side of a thing. It would have made more sense for them to be on Herod's side.

'Exactly,' Mother said. 'It was perfectly disgraceful. And I never thought about it much. You hear all about the nice warm stable with all the animals breathing, and the sweet-smelling hay – but that doesn't change the fact that they put Mary in a barn. Now, let me tell you . . .' She told my father all about the rehearsal and when she was through she said, 'It's clear to me that, deep down, those children have *some* good instincts after all.'

My father said he couldn't exactly agree. 'According to you,' he said, 'their chief instinct was to burn Herod alive.'

'No, their chief instinct was to get Mary and the baby out of the barn. But even so, it was *Herod* they wanted to do away with, and not Mary or Joseph. They picked out the right villain – that must mean something.'

'Maybe so.' My father looked up from his newspaper. 'Is that what finally happened to Herod? What *did* happen to Herod, anyway?'

None of us knew. I had never thought much about Herod. He was just a name, somebody in the Bible, Herod the king.

But the Herdmans went and looked him up.

The very next day Imogene grabbed me at recess. 'How do you get a book out of the library?' she said.

'You have to have a card.'

'How do you get a card?'

'You have to sign your name.'

She looked at me for a minute, with her eyes all squinched up. 'Do you have to sign your own name?'

I thought Imogene probably wanted to get one of the dirty books out of the basement, which is where they keep them, but I knew nobody would let her do that. There is this big chain across the stairs to the basement and Miss Graebner, the librarian, can hear it rattle no matter where she is in the library, so you don't stand a chance of getting down there.

'Sure you have to sign your own name,' I said. 'They have to know who has the books.' I didn't see what difference it made – whether she signed the card with her own name, or signed the card Queen Elizabeth – Miss Graebner still wasn't going to let Imogene Herdman take any books out of the public library.

I guess she couldn't stop them from using the library, though, because that was where they found out about Herod.

They went in that afternoon, all six of them, and told Miss Graebner that they wanted library cards. Usually when anybody told Miss Graebner that they wanted a library card, she got this big happy smile on her face and said, 'Good! We want all our boys and girls to have library cards.'

She didn't say that to the Herdmans, though. She just asked them *why* they wanted library cards.

'We want to read about Jesus,' Imogene said.

'Not Jesus,' Ralph said, 'that king who was out to get Jesus . . . Herod.'

Later on Miss Graebner told my mother that she had been a librarian for thirty-eight years and loved every minute of it because every day brought something new and different. 'But now,' she said, 'I might as well retire. When Imogene Herdman came in and said she wanted to read about Jesus, I knew I'd heard everything there was to hear.'

At the next rehearsal Mother started, again, to separate everyone into angels and shepherds and guests at the inn but she didn't get very far. The

Herdmans wanted to rewrite the whole pageant and hang Herod for a finish. They couldn't stand it that he died in bed of old age.

'It wasn't just Jesus he was after,' Ralph told us. 'He killed all kinds of people.'

'He even killed his own wife,' Leroy said.

'And nothing happened to him,' Imogene grumbled.

'Well, he died, didn't he?' somebody said. 'Maybe he died a horrible death. What did he die of?'

Ralph shrugged. 'It didn't say. Flu, I guess.'

They were so mad about it that I thought they might quit the pageant. But they didn't – not then or ever – and all the people who kept hoping that the Herdmans would get bored and leave were out of luck. They showed up at rehearsals, right on time, and did just what they were supposed to do.

But they were still Herdmans, and there was at least one person who didn't forget that for a minute.

One day I saw Alice Wendleken writing something down on a little pad of paper, and trying to hide it with her other hand.

'It's none of your business,' she said.

It *wasn't* any of my business, but it wasn't any of Alice's, either. What she wrote was 'Gladys Herdman drinks communion wine.'

'It isn't wine,' I said. 'It's grape juice.'

'I don't care what it is, she drinks it. I've seen her three times with her mouth all purple. They steal crayons from the Sunday-school cupboards, too, and if you shake the Happy Birthday bank in the kindergarten room it doesn't make a sound. They stole all the pennies out of that.'

I was amazed at Alice. I would never think to go and shake the Happy Birthday bank.

'And every time you go in the girls' room,' she went on, 'the whole air is blue, and Imogene Herdman is sitting there in the Mary costume, smoking cigars!'

Alice wrote all these things down, and how many times each thing happened. I don't know why, unless it made her feel good to see, in black and white, just how awful they were.

Since none of the Herdmans had ever gone to church or Sunday school or read the Bible or anything, they didn't know how things were supposed to be. Imogene, for instance, didn't know that Mary was supposed to be acted out in one certain way – sort of quiet and dreamy and out of this world.

The way Imogene did it, Mary was a lot like Mrs. Santoro at the Pizza Parlour. Mrs. Santoro is a big fat lady with a little skinny husband and nine children and she yells and hollers and hugs her kids and slaps them around. That's how Imogene's Mary was – loud and bossy.

'Get away from the baby!' she yelled at Ralph, who was Joseph. And she made the Wise Men keep their distance.

'The Wise Men want to honour the Christ Child,' Mother explained, for the tenth time. 'They don't mean to harm him, for heaven's sake!'

But the Wise Men didn't know how things were

supposed to be either, and nobody blamed Imogene for shoving them out of the way. You got the feeling that *these* Wise Men were going to hustle back to Herod as fast as they could and squeal on the baby, out of pure meanness.

They thought about it, too.

'What if we *didn't* go home another way?' Leroy demanded. Leroy was Melchior. 'What if we went back to the king and told on the baby – where he was and all?'

'He would murder Jesus,' Ralph said. 'Old Herod would murder him.'

'He would not!' That was Imogene, with fire in her eye, and since the Herdmans fought one another just as fast as they fought everybody else, Mother had to step in and settle everyone down.

I thought about it later though and I decided that if Herod, a king, set out to murder Jesus, a carpenter's baby son, he would surely find some way to do it. So when Leroy said 'What if we went back and told on the baby?' it gave you something to think about.

No Jesus . . . ever.

I don't know whether anybody else got this flash. Alice Wendleken, for one, didn't.

'I don't think it's very nice to talk about the baby Jesus being murdered,' she said, stitching her lips together and looking sour. That was one more thing to write down on her pad of paper, and one more thing to tell her mother about the Herdmans – besides the fact that they swore and smoked and stole and all. I think she kept hoping that they would do one great big sinful thing and her mother would say, 'Well, that's that!' and get on the telephone and have them thrown out.

'Be sure and tell your mother that I can step right in and be Mary if I have to,' she told me as we stood in the back row of the angel choir. 'And, if *I'm* Mary we can get the Perkins baby for Jesus. But Mrs. Perkins won't let Imogene Herdman get her hands on him.' The Perkins baby would have made a terrific Jesus, and Alice knew it.

The way things stood, we didn't have any baby at all – and this really bothered my mother because you couldn't very well have the best Christmas pageant in history with the chief character missing.

We had lots of babies offered in the beginning – all the way from Eugene Sloper who was so new he was still red, up to Junior Caudill who was almost four (his mother said he could scrunch up). But when all the mothers found out about the Herdmans they withdrew their babies.

Mother had called everybody she knew, trying to scratch up a baby, but the closest she came was Bernice Watrous, who kept foster babies all the time.

'I've got a darling little boy right now,' Bernice told Mother. 'He's three months old, and so good I hardly know he's in the house. He'd be wonderful. Of course he's Chinese. Does that matter?'

'No,' Mother said. 'It doesn't matter at all.'

But Bernice's baby got adopted two weeks before Christmas, and Bernice said she didn't like to ask to borrow him back right away.

So that was that.

'Listen,' Imogene said. 'I'll get us a baby.'

'How would you do that?' Mother asked.

'I'll steal one,' Imogene said. 'There's always two or three babies in carriages outside the A & P super-market.'

'Oh, Imogene, don't be ridiculous,' Mother said, 'You can't just walk off with somebody's baby, you know!' I doubt if Imogene *did* know that – she walked off with everything else.

'We just won't worry any more about a baby,' Mother said. 'We'll use a baby doll. That'll be better anyway.'

Imogene looked pleased. 'A doll can't bite you,' she pointed out. Which just went to prove that Herdmans started out mean, right from the cradle.

CHAPTER SIX

Our last rehearsal happened to be the night before the pot-luck supper, and when we got there the kitchen was full of ladies in aprons, counting out dishes and silverware and making applesauce cake for the dessert.

'I'm sorry about this,' one of the ladies told Mother, 'but with so much to do at this time of year, the committee decided to come in this evening and set up the tables and all. I just hope we won't bother you.'

'Oh, you won't,' Mother said. 'We won't be in the kitchen. You won't even know we're here.'

Mother was wrong – everybody in that end of town knew we were there before the evening was over.

'Now, this is going to be a dress rehearsal,' Mother told us all, and right away three or four baby angels began hollering that they forgot their wings. Half the angel choir had forgotten their robes, and Hobie Carmichael said he didn't have any kind of a costume.

'Wear your father's bathrobe,' Charlie told him. 'That's what I do.'

'He doesn't have a bathrobe.'

'What does he hang around the house in?'

'His underwear,' Hobie said.

I looked at Alice Wendleken to see if she was going to write that down on her pad of paper, but Alice was standing all by herself in a corner, patting her hair. Her hair was all washed and curled, and her robe was clean and pressed. She had even put vaseline on her eyelids, so they would shine in the candlelight and everyone would say 'Who is that lovely girl in the angel choir? Why isn't she Mary?' I guess Alice was afraid to move, for fear she might spoil herself.

'Don't worry about your wings,' Mother said. 'The main point of a dress rehearsal isn't the costumes. The main point is to go right straight through without stopping. And that's what we're going to do, just as if we were doing it for the whole congregation. I'm going to sit in the back of the church and be the audience.'

But it didn't work that way. The baby angels came in at the wrong place and had to go back out again, and a whole gang of shepherds didn't come in at all, for fear of Gladys. Imogene couldn't find the baby Jesus doll, and wrapped up a great big memorial flower urn in the blanket, and then dropped it on Ralph's foot. And half the angel choir sang 'Away in a Manger' while the other half sang 'O, Little Town of Bethlehem'.

So we had to keep starting again.

'I've got the baby here,' Imogene barked at the Wise Men. 'Don't touch him! I named him Jesus.'

'No, no, no.' Mother came flying up the aisle. 'Now, Imogene, you know you're not supposed to say anything. Nobody says anything in our pageant, except the Angel of the Lord and the choir singing carols. Mary and Joseph and the Wise Men make a lovely picture for us to look at while we think about Christmas and what it means.'

I guess Mother had to say things like that, even though everybody knew it was a big lie. The Herdmans didn't look like *anything* out of the Bible – more like trick-or-treat. Imogene even had on great big gold earrings, and she wouldn't take them off.

'Now, Imogene,' Mother said. 'You know Mary didn't wear earrings.'

'I have to wear these,' Imogene said.

'Why is that?'

'I got my ears pierced, and if I don't keep something in 'em, they'll grow together.'

'Well, they won't grow together in an hour and a half,' Mother said.

'No . . . but I better leave 'em in.' Imogene pulled on her earrings, which made you shudder – it was like looking at the pictures in *National Geographic* of natives with their ears stretched all the way to their shoulders.

'What did the doctor say about leaving something in them?' Mother said.

'What doctor?'

'Well, who pierced your ears?'

'Gladys,' Imogene said.

That really made you shudder – the thought of

Gladys Herdman piercing ears. I thought she probably used an ice pick, and for the next six months I kept watching Imogene, to see her ears turn black and fall off.

'All right,' Mother said, 'but we'll try to find something smaller and more appropriate for you to wear in the pageant. Now we'll start again and go right straight through, and – '

'I think I ought to tell them what his name is,' Imogene said.

'No. Besides, you remember it wasn't Mary who named the baby.'

'I told you!' Ralph whacked Imogene on the back. '*I* named him.'

'Joseph didn't name the baby either,' Mother said. 'God sent an angel to tell Mary what his name should be.'

Imogene sniffed. 'I would have named him Bill.'

Alice Wendleken sucked in her breath, and I could hear her scratching down on her pad of paper that Imogene Herdman would have called the baby Bill instead of Jesus.

'What angel was that?' Ralph wanted to know. 'Was that Gladys?'

'No,' Mother said. 'Gladys is the angel who comes to the shepherds with the news.'

'Yeh,' Gladys said. 'Unto you a child is born!' she yelled at the shepherds.

'Unto *me*!' Imogene yelled back at her. 'Not them, me! I'm the one that had the baby!'

'No, no, no.' Mother sat down on a front pew.

'That just means that Jesus belongs to everybody. Unto *all* of us a child is born. Now,' she sighed. 'Let's start again, and –'

'Why didn't they let Mary name her own baby?' Imogene demanded. 'What did that angel do, just walk up and say, "Name him Jesus"?'

'Yes,' Mother said, because she was in a hurry to get finished.

But Alice Wendleken had to open her big mouth. 'I know what the angel said,' Alice piped up. 'She said, "His name shall be called Wonderful, Counsellor, Mighty God, Everlasting Father, the Prince of Peace."'

I could have hit her.

'My God!' Imogene said. 'He'd never get out of the first grade if he had to write all that!'

There was a big crash at the back of the church, as if somebody dropped all the collection plates. But it wasn't the collection plates – it was Mrs. Hopkins, the minister's wife, dropping a whole tray of silverware.

'I'm sorry,' she said. 'I was just passing by, and I thought I'd take a peek . . .'

'Would you like to sit down and watch the rehearsal?' Mother asked.

'No-o-o.' Mrs. Hopkins couldn't seem to take her eyes off Imogene. 'I'd better go check on the applesauce cake.'

'You didn't have to say that,' I told Alice. 'All that about Wonderful, Everlasting Father, and all.'

'Why not?' Alice said, patting her hair. 'I thought Imogene wanted to know.'

By that time everyone was hot and tired, and most of the baby angels had to go to the bathroom, so Mother said we would take a five-minute recess. 'And then we'll start again,' she said, looking sort of hopeless, 'and go straight through without stopping, won't we?'

Well, we never did go right straight through. The five-minute recess was a big mistake, because it stretched to fifteen minutes, and Imogene spent the whole time smoking cigars in one of the johns in the ladies' room. Then Mrs. Homer McCarthy went to the ladies' room and opened the door and smelled something funny and saw some smoke – and she ran right to the church office and called the fire department.

We were singing 'Angels We Have Heard on High' when what we heard was the fire engine, pulling up on the lawn of the church, with the siren blaring and the red lights flashing. The firemen hurried in and made us all go outside, and they dragged a big hose in the front door and went looking for a fire to put out.

The street was full of baby angels crying, and shepherds climbing all over the fire truck, and firemen, and all the ladies on the pot-luck committee, and neighbours who came to see what was going on, and Reverend Hopkins who ran over from the parsonage in his pyjamas and his woolly bathrobe.

Nobody knew what had happened, including the

Herdmans, but I guess they figured that whatever it was, they had done it, so they left.

'Why in the world did you call the fire department?' Mother asked Mrs. McCarthy, when she finally heard the whole story.

'Because the ladies' room was full of thick smoke!'

'It couldn't have been,' Mother said. 'You just got excited. Didn't you know it was cigar smoke?'

Mrs. McCarthy stared at her. 'No, I didn't. I don't expect to find cigar smoke in the ladies' room of the church!' She whirled around and marched back to the kitchen.

But by that time the kitchen was fuller of smoke than the ladies' room, because, while everybody was milling around in the street, all the applesauce cake burned up.

Of course the ladies on the pot-luck committee were mad about that. Mrs. McCarthy was mad, and Alice said her mother would be good and mad when she heard about it. Most of the baby angels' mothers were mad because they couldn't find out what had happened – and somebody said Mrs. Hopkins was mad because Reverend Hopkins was running around the streets in his pyjamas.

It turned out to be the one great big sinful thing Alice kept hoping for.

Mrs. Wendleken read Alice's notes, got on the telephone that very night and called up everybody she could think of in the Ladies' Aid and the Women's Society. And she called most of the flower committee, and all the Sunday-school teachers, and Reverend Hopkins.

And Reverend Hopkins came to see Mother. 'I can't make head or tail of it,' he said. 'Some people say they set fire to the ladies' room. Some people say they set fire to the kitchen. One lady told me that Imogene threw a flower pot at Ralph. Mrs. Wendleken says all they do is talk about sex and underwear.'

'That was Hobie Carmichael,' Mother said, 'talking about underwear. And they didn't set fire to anything. The only fire was in the kitchen, where the pot-luck committee let their applesauce cake burn up.'

'Well . . .' Reverend Hopkins looked unhappy. 'The whole church is in an uproar. Do you think we should call off the pageant?'

'Certainly not!' Mother said. By that time she was mad, too. 'Why, it's going to be the best Christmas pageant we've ever had!'

Of all the lies she'd told so far, that was the biggest, but you had to admire her. It was like General Custer saying, 'Bring on the Indians!'

'Maybe so,' Reverend Hopkins said. 'I'm just afraid that no one will come to see it.'

But he was wrong.

Everybody came . . . to see what the Herdmands would do.

CHAPTER SEVEN

On the night of the pageant we didn't have any supper because Mother forgot to fix it. My father said that was all right. Between Mrs. Armstrong's telephone calls and the pageant rehearsals, he didn't expect supper any more.

'When it's all over,' he said, 'we'll go someplace and have hamburgers.' But Mother said when it was all over she might want to go some place and hide.

'We've never once gone through the whole thing,' she said. 'I don't know what's going to happen. It may be the first Christmas pageant in history where Joseph and the Wise Men get in a fight, and Mary runs away with the baby.'

She might be right, I thought, and I wondered what all of us in the angel choir ought to do in case that happened. It would be dumb for us just to stand there singing about the Holy Infant if Mary had run off with him.

But nothing seemed very different at first.

There was the usual big mess all over the place – baby angels getting poked in the eye by other baby angels' wings and grumpy shepherds stumbling over their bathrobes. The spotlight swooped back and forth and up and down till it made you sick at your stomach to look at it and, as usual, whoever was playing the piano pitched 'Away in a Manger' so high we could hardly hear it, let alone sing it. My father says 'Away in a Manger' always starts out sounding like a closetful of mice.

But everything settled down, and at 7.30 the pageant began.

While we sang 'Away in a Manger', the ushers lit candles all around the church, and the spotlight came on to be the star. So you really had to know the words to 'Away in a Manger' because you couldn't see anything – not even Alice Wendleken's vaseline eyelids.

After that we sang two verses of 'O, Little Town of Bethlehem', and then we were supposed to hum some more 'O, Little Town of Bethlehem' while Mary and Joseph came in from a side door. Only they didn't come right away. So we hummed and hummed and hummed, which is boring and also very hard, and before long doesn't sound like any song at all – more like an old refrigerator.

'I knew something like this would happen,' Alice Wendleken whispered to me. 'They didn't come at all! We won't have any Mary and Joseph – and now what are we supposed to do?'

I guess we would have gone on humming till we all turned blue, but we didn't have to. Ralph and Imogene were there all right, only for once they didn't come through the door pushing each other out of the way. They just stood there for a minute as if they weren't sure they were in the right place – because of the candles, I guess, and the church being full of people. They looked like the people you see on the six o'clock news – refugees, sent to wait in some strange ugly place, with all their boxes and sacks around them.

It suddenly occurred to me that this was just the way it must have been for the real Holy Family, stuck away in a barn by people who didn't much care what happened to them. They couldn't have been very neat and tidy either, but more like *this* Mary and Joseph (Imogene's veil was cockeyed as usual, and Ralph's hair stuck out all around his ears). Imogene had the baby doll but she wasn't carrying it the way she was supposed to, cradled in her arms. She had it slung up over her shoulder, and before she put it in the manger she thumped it twice on the back.

I heard Alice gasp and she poked me. 'I don't think it's very nice to burp the baby Jesus,' she whispered, 'as if he had colic.' Then she poked me again. 'Do you suppose he could have had colic?'

I said, 'I don't know why not,' and I didn't. He *could* have had colic, or been fussy, or hungry like any other baby. After all, that was the whole point of Jesus – that he didn't come down on a cloud like something out of 'Amazing Comics', but that he was born and lived . . . a real person.

Right away we had to sing 'While Shepherds Watched Their Flocks by Night' – and we had to sing very loud, because there were more shepherds than there were anything else, and they made so

66

much noise, banging their crooks around like a lot of hockey sticks.

Next came Gladys, from behind the angel choir, pushing people out of the way and stepping on everyone's feet. Since Gladys was the only one in the pageant who had anything to say she made the most of it: 'Hey! Unto you a child is born!' she hollered, as if it was, for sure, the best news in the world. And all the shepherds trembled, sore afraid – of Gladys, mainly, but it looked good anyway.

Then came three carols about angels. It took that long to get the angels in because they were all primary kids and they got nervous and cried and forgot where they were supposed to go and bent their wings in the door and things like that.

We got a little rest then, while the boys sang 'We Three Kings of Orient Are', and everybody in the audience shifted around to watch the Wise Men march up the aisle.

'What have they got?' Alice whispered.

I didn't know, but whatever it was, it was heavy – Leroy almost dropped it. He didn't have his frankincense jar either, and Claude and Ollie didn't have anything although they were supposed to bring the gold and the myrrh.

'I knew this would happen,' Alice said for the second time. 'I bet it's something awful.'

'Like what?'

'Like . . . a burnt offering. You know the Herdmans.'

Well, they did burn things, but they hadn't burned

this yet. It was a ham – and right away I knew where it came from. My father was on the church charitable works committee – they give away food baskets at Christmas, and this was the Herdman's food-basket ham. It still had the ribbon around it, saying Merry Christmas.

'I'll bet they stole that!' Alice said.

'They did not. It came from their food basket, and if they want to give away their own ham I guess they can do it.' But even if the Herdmans didn't *like* ham (that was Alice's next idea) they had never before in their lives given anything away except lumps on the head. So you had to be impressed.

Leroy dropped the ham in front of the manger. It looked funny to see a ham there instead of the fancy bathsalts jars we always used for the myrrh and the frankincense. And then they went and sat down in the only space that was left.

While we sang 'What Child Is This?' the Wise Men were supposed to confer among themselves and then leave by a different door, so everyone would understand that they were going home another way. But the Herdmans forgot, or didn't want to, or something, because they didn't confer and they didn't leave either. They just sat there, and there wasn't anything anyone could do about it.

'They're ruining the whole thing!' Alice whispered, but they weren't at all. As a matter of fact, it made perfect sense for the Wise Men to sit down and rest, and I said so.

'They're supposed to have come a long way. You

wouldn't expect them just to show up, hand over the ham, and leave!'

As for ruining the whole thing, it seemed to me that the Herdmans had improved the pageant a lot, just by doing what came naturally – like burping the baby, for instance, or thinking a ham would make a better present than a lot of perfumed oil.

Usually, by the time we got to 'Silent Night', which was always the last carol, I was fed up with the whole thing and couldn't wait for it to be over. But I didn't feel that way this time. I almost wished for the pageant to go on, with the Herdmans in charge, to see what else they would do that was different.

Maybe the Wise Men would tell Mary about their problem with Herod, and she would tell them to go back and lie their heads off. Or Joseph might go with them and get rid of Herod once and for all. Or Joseph and Mary might ask the Wise Men to take the Christ Child with them, figuring that no one would think to look there.

I was so busy planning new ways to save the baby Jesus that I missed the beginning of 'Silent Night', but it was all right because everyone sang 'Silent Night', including the audience. We sang all the verses too, and when we got to 'Son of God, Love's pure light' I happened to look at Imogene and I almost dropped my hymn book on a baby angel.

Everyone had been waiting all this time for the Herdmans to do something absolutely unexpected. And sure enough, that was what happened.

Imogene Herdman was crying.

In the candlelight her face was all shiny with tears and she didn't even bother to wipe them away. She just sat there – awful old Imogene – in her crookedy veil, crying and crying and crying.

Well. It *was* the best Christmas pageant we ever had.

Everybody said so, but nobody seemed to know why. When it was over people stood around the lobby of the church talking about what was different this year. There was something special, everyone said – they couldn't put their finger on what.

Mrs. Wendleken said, 'Well, Mary the mother of Jesus had a black eye; that was something special. But only what you might expect,' she added.

She meant that it was the most natural thing in the world for a Herdman to have a black eye. But actually nobody hit Imogene and she didn't hit anyone else. Her eye wasn't really black either, just all puffy and swollen. She had walked into the corner of the choir-robe cabinet, in a kind of daze – as if she had just caught on to the idea of God, and the wonder of Christmas.

And this was the funny thing about it all. For years, I'd thought about the wonder of Christmas, and the mystery of Jesus' birth, and never really understood it. But now, because of the Herdmans, it didn't seem so mysterious after all.

When Imogene had asked me what the pageant was about, I told her it was about Jesus, but that was just part of it. It was about a new baby, and his mother and father who were in a lot of trouble – no money, no place to go, no doctor, nobody they knew. And then, arriving from the East (like my uncle from New Jersey) some rich friends.

But Imogene, I guess, didn't see it that way. Christmas just came over her all at once, like a case of chills and fever. And so she was crying, and walking into the furniture.

Afterwards there were candy canes and little tiny Testaments for everyone, and a poinsettia plant for my mother from the whole Sunday school. We put the costumes away and folded up the collapsible manger, and just before we left, my father snuffed out the last of the tall white candles.

'I guess that's everything,' he said as we stood at the back of the church. 'All over now. It was quite a pageant.' Then he looked at my mother. 'What's that you've got?'

'It's the ham,' she said. 'They wouldn't take it back. They wouldn't take any candy either, or any of the little Bibles. But Imogene did ask me for a set of the Bible-story pictures, and she took out the Mary picture and said it was exactly right, whatever that means.'

I think it meant that no matter how she herself was, Imogene liked the idea of the Mary in the picture – all pink and white and pure-looking, as if she never washed the dishes or cooked supper or did anything at all except have Jesus on Christmas Eve.

But as far as I'm concerned, Mary is always going to look a lot like Imogene Herdman – sort of nervous and bewildered, but ready to clobber anyone who laid a hand on her baby. And the Wise Men are always going to be Leroy and his brothers, bearing ham.

When we came out of the church that night it was cold and clear, with crunchy snow underfoot and bright, bright stars overhead. And I thought about the Angel of the Lord – Gladys, with her skinny legs and her dirty sneakers sticking out from under her robe, yelling at all of us, everywhere:

'Hey! Unto you a child is born!'

THE WORST KIDS IN
THE WORLD

THE BEST SCHOOL
YEAR EVER

Barbara Robinson

THE HERDMANS . . . BACK AGAIN!

When we studied the Old West, everybody had to do a special report on A Cowboy's Life or Famous Indian Chiefs or Notorious Outlaw Families like the James brothers. Boomer Malone picked the James brothers, but then he couldn't find them in the children's encyclopedia.

'That's all right, Boomer,' Miss Kemp said. 'It doesn't have to be the James brothers. Pick another outlaw family.'

So Boomer did. He picked the Herdmans.

Of course, the Herdmans weren't in the Old West, and they weren't in the children's encyclopedia either. They were right there in the Woodrow Wilson School, all six of them spread out, one to a class, because the only teacher who could put up with two of them at once would have to be a Miss King Kong. My father said he bet that was in the teachers' contracts along with sick leave and medical benefits: only one Herdman at a time.

Boomer's paper was the best one, three whole pages of one crime after another. He should have gotten A plus, but Miss Kemp made him do the whole paper over.

'I'm ashamed of you, Boomer,' she said, 'calling your own schoolmates an outlaw family.'

The Herdmans didn't care. They knew they were outlaws. So did Miss Kemp, but I guess she had to pretend they were like everybody else.

They weren't, and if they *had* been around in the Old West, they would have burned it all down or blown it all up and we wouldn't have to study about it.

Plus, of course, we wouldn't have to live with Herdmans every day, in school and out. . . .

CHAPTER ONE

Unless you're somebody like Huckleberry Finn, the first day of school isn't too bad. Most kids, by then, are bored with summer and itchy from mosquito bites and poison ivy and nothing to do. Your sneakers are all worn out and you can't get new ones till school starts and your mother is sick and tired of yelling at you to pick things up and you're sick and tired of picking the same things up.

Plus, the first day of school is only half a day for kids.

My little brother, Charlie, once asked my mother what the teachers do for the rest of the day.

'They get things ready – books and papers and lessons.'

'That's not what Leroy Herdman says,' Charlie told her. 'Leroy says as soon as the kids are gone, they lock all the doors and order in pizza and beer.'

'Well, they don't,' Mother said, 'and how would Leroy know anyway?'

'He forgot something,' Charlie said, 'and he went back to get it and he couldn't get in.'

'They saw him coming and locked the doors,' Mother said. 'Wouldn't you?'

Well, yes. Anyone would, because the Herdmans – Ralph, Imogene, Leroy, Claude, Ollie, and Gladys – were the worst kids in the history of the world. They weren't honest or cheerful or industrious or cooperative or clean. They told lies and smoked cigars and set fire to things and hit little kids and cursed and stayed away from school whenever they wanted to and wouldn't learn anything when they were there.

They were always there, though, on the first day, so you always knew right away that this was going to be another exciting Herdman year in the Woodrow Wilson Elementary School.

At least there was only one of them in each grade, and since they never got kept back, you always had the same one to put up with. I had Imogene, and what I did was stay out of her way, but it wasn't easy.

This time she grabbed me in the hall and shoved an oatmeal box in my face. 'Hey,' she said, 'you want to buy a science project?'

I figured that Imogene's idea of a science project would probably explode or catch fire or smell really bad or be alive and bite me – and, in fact, I could hear something squealing and scratching around in the oatmeal box.

'Miss Kemp already wrote this year's assignment on the board,' I said, 'and it isn't a science project.'

'Fine time to tell me,' Imogene grunted. 'What is it? The assignment.' She shook her oatmeal box. 'Is it mice?'

So I was half right – Imogene's science project was

alive, but it probably wouldn't bite me unless it was great big mice, and I didn't want to find out.

'No,' I said, 'it's about people.'

'Mice would be better,' Imogene said.

Later that morning Miss Kemp explained her assignment, and I thought Imogene might be right, because the assignment sounded weird.

'For this year's project,' she said, 'we're going to study each other. That's the assignment on the blackboard, Compliments for Classmates.'

All over the room hands were going up and kids were saying 'Huh?' and 'What does it mean?' and 'How many pages?' But Miss Kemp ignored all this.

'It means exactly what it says,' she said. 'You're to think of a special compliment for each person in this class, and please don't groan' – a lot of people did anyway – 'because this is the assignment for the *year*. You have all year to think about it, and next June, before the last day of school, you'll draw names from a hat and think of more compliments for just that one person.'

Somebody asked if it could be a famous person instead, and somebody else asked if it could be a dead famous person, like George Washington.

Miss Kemp said no. 'This is a classroom project, so it has to be people in this class. We know all about George Washington's good points, but . . .' She looked around and picked on Boomer. 'We don't know all Boomer's good points. More important, *Boomer* probably doesn't know all his good points.'

'How many compliments?' Junior Jacobs wanted to know.

'Up to you,' Miss Kemp said.

Alice Wendleken raised her hand. 'Would beautiful hair and shiny hair count as one compliment?'

This sounded to me as if Alice planned to compliment herself, which would save someone else the trouble, but Miss Kemp said, 'I'm not talking about beautiful hair and nice teeth, Alice. I mean characteristics, personal qualities, something special.'

This could be hard, I thought. Take Albert Pelfrey. When you think of Albert Pelfrey, you think *fat*. Even Albert thinks *fat*. It's hard to think anything else, so I would really have to study Albert to find some special personal quality that wasn't just about being fat. And besides Albert there were twenty-eight other people, including Imogene Herdman.

'What's a compliment?' Imogene asked me.

'It's something nice you tell someone, like if someone is especially helpful or especially friendly.'

Alice looked Imogene up and down. 'Or especially clean,' she said.

'Okay.' Imogene frowned. 'But mice would still be better.'

Mice would probably be *easier* for Imogene because the Herdmans always had animals around. As far as I know they weren't mean to the animals, but the animals they weren't mean to were mean all by themselves, like their cat, which was crazy and had to be kept on a chain because it bit people.

Now and then you would see Mrs. Herdman walking the cat around the block on its chain, but she worked two shifts at the shoe factory and didn't have much time left over to hang around the house and walk the cat.

There wasn't any Mr. Herdman. Everybody agreed that after Gladys was born, he just climbed on a freight train and left town, but some people said he did it right away and some people said he waited a year or two.

'Gladys probably bit him,' my friend Alice Wendleken said.

'Not if she was a baby?' I asked. 'Babies don't have any teeth.'

'She probably had hard, hard gums.' Alice knew what she was talking about, because Gladys bit her all the time. Mrs. Wendleken always poured iodine all over the bites, so Alice had to go around for days with big brown splotches on her arms and legs. Alice was always afraid she would die anyway (of Gladysbite) and have to be buried looking splotched up and ugly instead of beautiful in her blue-and-white dress with the ruffles.

It wasn't all that special to get bitten by Gladys. She bit everybody, including my little brother, Charlie. Charlie came home yelling and screaming that Gladys bit him, and Gladys came too, which shows you how fearless they were. Any other kid who bit a kid and broke the skin and drew blood would go hide somewhere, but not Gladys.

'Gladys Herdman!' It's always your whole name

when my mother is mad. 'Do you know what I think about a little girl who bites people? I think she ought to have to wear a sign around her neck that says "Beware of Gladys."'

I guess Mother thought that would really put Gladys in her place, but Gladys just said 'Okay' and went home and made the sign and wore it for a week. Nobody paid much attention – we didn't need a sign to make us beware of Gladys.

Besides everything else they did, the Herdmans would steal anything they could carry, and it was surprising what all they could carry – not just candy and gum and gerbils and goldfish. They even stole Mrs. Johanneson's concrete birdbath, for the goldfish, I guess. And last spring they stole my friend Louella McCluskey's baby brother, Howard, from in front of the grocery store.

Of course Howard wasn't supposed to be in front of the grocery store. Louella was supposed to be baby-sitting him, which she did every Tuesday afternoon while her mother went to the beauty parlour. Louella got paid fifty cents to do this, and on that particular Tuesday we were in the grocery store spending her fifty cents.

When we came out – no Howard. The stroller was still there, though, and that's why we didn't think of the Herdmans right away. Usually if you missed something, you would just naturally figure the Herdmans had it. But when they stole a thing, they always stole all of the thing. It wasn't like them to take the baby and leave the stroller.

Louella turned the stroller over and looked underneath it as if she thought Howard might have fallen through, which was pretty dumb. Then we walked up and down the street, hollering for Howard, which was also dumb. How could Howard answer? He couldn't even talk. He couldn't walk either, or crawl very much. He couldn't get out of the stroller in the first place.

'Well, somebody must have taken him,' Louella said. 'Some stranger has just walked off with my baby brother.'

'You better tell a policeman,' I said.

'No, I don't want to. They would get my mother out of the beauty parlour and I don't want her to know.'

'She'll know when you come home without Howard,' I said.

'I won't go home. Not till I find him. Now let's just think. Who would take Howard?'

I couldn't imagine who would take Howard. Even my mother said Howard was the homeliest baby she'd ever laid eyes on, but she did say that he would probably be just fine once he grew some hair. That was his main trouble – having no hair. Here he was, bald as an egg, and Mrs. McCluskey kept rubbing his head with Vaseline to make the hair grow. So when you looked at Howard, all you saw was this shiny white head. Not too good.

'Probably someone who just loves babies,' Louella said, but that could be anybody. It would be easier to think of someone who hates babies, but if you hated them you certainly wouldn't steal one.

Then Louella had another idea. 'Let's just walk down the street,' she said, 'pushing the stroller. Maybe someone has seen Howard and when they see us with an empty stroller they'll figure we're looking for him and tell us where he is.'

I was pretty disgusted. 'Louella,' I said, 'you know that won't happen.'

But it did. The first person we met was my little brother, Charlie, and the first thing he said was, 'If you're looking for Howard, the Herdmans have got him.'

Louella looked relieved, but not very, and I didn't blame her. If you had to choose between a total stranger having your baby brother and the Herdmans having him, you would pick the total stranger every time.

'What have they done with him?' Louella asked.

'They're charging kids a quarter to look at him.'

'Why would anybody pay a quarter to look at Howard?' I said. 'We can look at Howard anytime.'

'They don't tell you it's Howard. They've got a sign up that says, "See the Amazing Tattooed Baby! 25 cents."'

'They tattooed him!' Louella yelped. 'My mother will kill me!'

Actually, they didn't tattoo him. What they did was wipe off the Vaseline and draw pictures all over his head with waterproof marker.

Charlie was dumb enough to fall for their sign. He

paid his quarter to see an amazing tattooed baby, and of course he was mad as could be when it turned out to be Howard McCluskey with pictures drawn all over his head.

So he tagged along behind us, insisting that Louella get his money back, but we both knew that Louella would have all she could do just to get Howard back.

'If it was anything but the baby,' she said, 'I wouldn't even *try* to get it back – not from the Herdmans.'

'They already collected six-fifty,' Charlie said. 'You ought to make them pay you some of that for the use of Howard.'

'I'll probably have to pay them,' Louella grumbled.

She was right. When we got to the Herdmans', there were three or four kids lined up outside the fence, and Louella marched up and said to Imogene Herdman, 'You give me back my baby brother!'

But Imogene pretended not to hear her and just went on collecting money. 'You want to see the tattooed baby?' She jiggled the money box at Louella. 'It'll cost you a quarter.'

'It's no tattooed baby,' Louella said, 'it's my little brother.'

Imogene squinched her eyes together. 'How do you know?'

'I just know.'

'You do not. It could be anybody's baby. It could be some baby you never heard of. It'll cost you a quarter to find out.'

Sure enough, it was Howard and he was a sight. The whole top of his head was red and green and blue and purple with pictures of dogs and cats and trees and tic-tac-toe games.

'I don't know what you're so mad about,' Leroy Herdman said. 'He looks a lot better than he did.'

In a way Leroy was right. Howard looked a lot more *interesting*, but nobody expected Mrs. McCluskey to think so.

We took Howard out back of my house and tried to wash off his head, which is how we found out the pictures were all waterproof.

'Now what'll I do?' Louella asked.

'Tell your mother the Herdmans did it,' Charlie said.

'She'll just want to know why I let them do it, and how they got hold of him in the first place. Maybe we should use some soap.'

We tried all kinds of things on Howard, but the only thing that worked at all was scouring powder, and that didn't work too well. It made his head gritty and it didn't take off all the purple.

'If you don't stand too close to him,' Louella said, 'and then squint your eyes . . . does the purple look to you like veins?'

It didn't to me. 'But after all,' I told Louella, 'I *know* what it is. Your mother doesn't know what it is, so maybe it will look like veins to her.'

It didn't. Mrs. McCluskey was so mad that she got a sick headache and spots before her eyes and had to lie down for two days. The first thing she did after she got up was go to work on Howard's head to try and get the purple off, and she discovered two or three patches of soft fuzz.

So then she wasn't mad at the Herdmans anymore. She said that something about all the drawing or the Magic Marker ink must have started his hair to grow. But she was still mad at Louella, which didn't seem fair. After all, it *could* have been the scouring powder.

I said that to my mother, and I knew right away that it was a mistake, because she said, 'What scouring powder?' and then, 'Beth Bradley, come back here! What scouring powder?'

So then I got punished for putting scouring powder on Howard's head, and Louella got punished for leaving him in front of the grocery store, and Charlie got punished by not having any Choco-Whoopee bars from the ice cream man till next week.

'That's what your quarter was for,' Mother told him. 'Next time you'll think twice before you throw away your quarter on something silly.'

Of course, Howard got some hair, but he was just a baby and he didn't care whether he had any hair or not. The Herdmans, who caused all the trouble in the first place, got $6.50.

If anybody but the Herdmans had stolen a baby and scribbled all over his head and then charged people money to look at him, they would have been shut up in the house for the rest of their natural lives. But since it *was* the Herdmans, most people just said how lucky Mrs. McCluskey was to get Howard back all in one piece, and that was that.

The truth is that no one wanted to fool around with them, so you knew that unless they tried to hold up the First National Bank or burn down the public library, you weren't going to see the last of them – especially if you had to go to the Woodrow Wilson School, and be in the same class with Imogene, and figure out something good to say about her before the end of the year.

CHAPTER TWO

A lot of people, like Alice Wendleken's mother, thought the Herdmans ought to be in jail, kids or not, but I knew that wouldn't happen.

Our jail is just two cells in the basement of the town hall, and the Herdmans aren't allowed in the town hall anymore since Gladys and Ollie put all the frogs in the drinking fountain there. They were little tiny frogs, and Miss Farley, the town clerk, drank two or three of them off the top of the bubbler by mistake. She didn't have her glasses on, she said, and didn't see them till somebody hollered, 'Evelyn, stop! You're drinking frogs!'

Miss Farley was hysterical! She said she could feel them jerking and jumping all up and down her wind-pipe. But even so she chased Gladys and Ollie all around the block, and she said if she ever caught any Herdmans inside the town hall again, she would put on roller skates and run them out of town so fast their heels would smoke.

Of course they didn't care. 'What'd she eat our frogs for anyway?' Gladys said. 'It's not our fault she ate our frogs. She'll get warts in her stomach, where she can't scratch them.'

'Warts don't itch,' Alice Wendleken told her.

'These will,' Gladys said. 'We caught the frogs in a patch of poison ivy.'

The town hall wasn't the only place in town where the Herdmans weren't allowed in to get a drink of water or go to the bathroom or call their mother or anything. They also weren't allowed in the drugstore or the movie theatre or the A&P or the Tasti-Lunch Diner.

They used to be allowed in the post office, but that didn't last. Somebody got hold of all their school pictures and put them up right next to the 'WANTED' posters, and it seemed so natural for them to be there that nobody noticed till Ollie Herdman went up and asked the postmaster, Mr. Blair, how much money he could get for his brother Claude.

'I don't know what you mean,' Mr. Blair said.

'Some of those people are worth five hundred dollars,' Ollie said. 'How much can I get for Claude?'

So Mr. Blair went to see what he was talking about and sure enough, there were the Herdmans right up with the bank robbers and the mad bombers and all.

Mr. Blair had a fit. 'How did these pictures get up here?' he said. 'Did you put these pictures up here?'

Ollie said no, it was a big surprise to him.

'Well, it's a big surprise to me too,' Mr. Blair said, 'but I can tell you that the FBI is not going to pay you anything for Claude, or any of the rest of you either. How did you happen to pick on Claude?'

'Because he's the one I've got,' Ollie said.

Mr. Blair said later that he didn't like the sound of that. 'I figured he probably had Claude tied to a tree somewhere.' So he mentioned it to the policeman on the corner, and the policeman said he'd better go investigate because with Herdmans you never could tell.

He didn't have to go far. There was a big crowd of people and a lot of commotion halfway down the block, and sure enough, Ollie had shut Claude up in the men's room of the Sunoco station.

When the policeman got there, Claude was banging on the door and hollering for someone to let him out, and there was a whole big family from South Dakota wanting to get in. The mother said they had driven almost a hundred and fifty miles looking for a Sunoco station because they were the cleanest, but what good was clean if you couldn't get in?

'I gave the key to one of those Herdmans,' the manager said, 'and he went off with it. I should have my head examined.'

'But you don't need a key to get *out*,' the policeman said. 'Why doesn't Claude just open the door?'

'I can't,' Claude yelled. 'The door's stuck.'

Ollie claimed later that he didn't have anything to do with that; that he hadn't even planned to shut Claude up in the men's room or anywhere else, but when the door jammed shut he went off to get help, and that was when he saw the pictures at the post office.

'You were going to get help at the post office?' the manager asked.

'I was going to get my sister Imogene.'

'And she was at the post office?'

'No,' Ollie said, 'she wasn't there.'

That was typical Herdman – there was a lie in it somewhere, but you couldn't put your finger on where.

Of course all that was later. In the meantime Mr. Blair and the Sunoco station manager had to get the fire department to break in the door and get Claude out. By that time the South Dakota people had left, and a lot of other people who wanted gas got tired of waiting and went somewhere else, and in all the excitement somebody walked off with two cans of motor oil and a wrench. Herdmans, probably, but nobody could prove it, just like nobody could prove that Ollie really meant to hand Claude over to the FBI for money.

So then the Herdmans weren't allowed in the post office *or* the Sunoco station, and they got thrown out of the new Laundromat the very day it opened.

They planned to wash their cat in one of the machines, but they didn't know it would cost money, so they just dropped him in and went off to locate some quarters.

Of course the cat didn't like it in the washing machine, and it made so much noise hissing and spitting and scratching that the manager, Mr. Cleveland, went to see what was wrong.

'I thought it was a short circuit,' he said, 'or a loose

connection – something electrical. That's the kind of noise it was.'

People said it *looked* electrical, all right. When he opened the lid, the cat shot out with its tail and its ears and all its hair standing straight up. It skittered around all over the tops of the machines and clawed through everybody's laundry baskets, and knocked over boxes of soap and bottles of bleach and a big basket of flowers that said 'Good Luck to the Laundromat'.

Finally someone opened the door, and the last they saw of the cat it was roaring down the street, all tangled up in a tablecloth.

Of course the Laundromat was a mess and all the customers were mad and couldn't find their clothes and wanted their money back for the stuff the cat had spilled. Pretty soon people began to sneeze from all the cat hair and soap powder in the air, and one lady broke out in big red blotches all over because she was allergic to cats. Mr. Cleveland sent everyone outdoors till things settled down.

But things didn't settle down. Santoro's Pizza Parlour was across the street, and when Mr. Santoro saw all these people coming out of the Laundromat sneezing and coughing and choking, he yelled, 'What's the matter? Is it a fire?'

Somebody yelled back, 'No – cat hair.' But Mr. Santoro thought they said 'bad air'. He figured there was something wrong with the new plumbing connections, maybe a gas leak, and he ran to the top of the street to warn people away in case of an explosion.

Some of the people he warned away were Herdmans – Imogene and Ralph and Leroy, on their way back with fifty cents for the washing machine.

'You children get away from here!' he said. 'The Laundromat may explode!'

I guess they were pretty surprised. They probably figured the cat did it, but they didn't know how. They also probably figured that if the cat was smart enough to blow up a Laundromat, it was smart enough to get away. So they just left.

Mr. Santoro called the fire department too and they came right away. But of course there wasn't any fire and there wasn't any gas leak, and by that time there wasn't any cat and there weren't any Herdmans either, just a lot of angry customers and a reporter from the newspaper who went around interviewing everybody.

Most of the people didn't even know what had happened because it happened so fast, so the newspaper story was pretty mysterious. 'LAUNDROMAT OPENING MARRED BY UNUSUAL DISTURBANCE', it said. 'FIREMEN RESPOND TO ANONYMOUS ALARM. CUSTOMERS DESCRIBE WILD ANIMAL'. My father said at least they got that part right.

Mr. Cleveland had to clean up the mess and replace everybody's stuff and pay for the blotched-up lady to get an allergy shot, so he was pretty mad. Mr. Santoro was mad because they called him 'anonymous', and of course the firemen were mad because they knew the Herdmans did it, whatever it was.

In the meantime the Herdmans were home, waiting for the cat to show up. The cat, crazier than usual because it was all wrapped up in a tablecloth, was tearing all over town, yowling and spitting and scratching at anything that got in its way.

It ran in the barber shop and streaked up one side of the chair where Mr. Perry was shaving someone.

'All of a sudden,' Mr. Perry said, 'there was a cat. So I lathered the cat by mistake. Missed my customer and lathered the cat.'

Then the cat ran through the lobby of the movie theatre and picked up some popcorn there, and by that time you couldn't tell what it was or what it had *ever* been.

It finally clawed its way up a tree in front of the library, and the librarian, Miss Graebner, called the fire department to come and get it down.

'I think it's a cat,' she said, 'and it looks like it's been through a war.'

'No,' the fire chief said, 'it's been through a washing machine, and as far as I'm concerned it can stay in that tree till the middle of next year.' Of course, Miss Graebner was mad about that.

The only people who weren't mad were the Herdmans, because when the cat finally came home, it was all clean and fluffy from the shaving lather, and that's what they wanted in the first place.

CHAPTER THREE

Naturally my mother wasn't too crazy about the Herdmans since they were always mopping up the floor with Charlie, but she had too much to do, she said, to spend time complaining about them – she would leave that to Alice Wendleken's mother, who was so good at it.

Mrs. Wendleken complained about them all the time, to everybody. It was her second favourite subject, besides how smart Alice was, and how pretty, and how talented, and how it would all go to waste if Gladys Herdman bit her to death.

Every time you turned around, Mrs. Wendleken was volunteering Alice to be the star of something – the main fairy or the head elf or the Clean Up Our Streets poster girl – and when the Chamber of Commerce bought a respirator for the hospital they put a picture of it in the paper and, sure enough, there was Alice hooked up to the respirator.

Mrs. Wendleken said she didn't have anything to do with that. The photographer just looked around and said, 'I wonder if that pretty little girl would be willing to pose with the respirator.' But nobody believed her.

Alice didn't get any applause for this either, but she carried the picture around anyway, and showed it to anyone who would hold still. She showed it to Imogene Herdman at recess, and Imogene took one look and hollered, 'Get away from me! Don't touch me! Whatever you've got, I don't want it!' – which brought the school nurse in a hurry in case Alice had smallpox or something.

It emptied the playground in a hurry too. Everybody figured that if it was something Imogene Herdman was scared to catch, it would wipe out the rest of us because ordinary germs didn't even slow the Herdmans down. They never got mumps or pinkeye or colds or stomachaches or anything. A snake once bit Leroy Herdman and Leroy's leg swelled up a little bit, but that was all.

The snake died. Leroy brought it to school and tied it all up and down the light cord in the teachers' supply closet, and about five minutes later the kindergarten teacher, Miss Newman, came in and pulled the cord.

She had all the day's helpers with her – six kindergarten kids carrying pots of red finger paint – and when Miss Newman screamed, they all dropped their pots and finger paint flew all over the place.

Then somebody upset two big boxes of chalk and they all tramped around in that, and when the janitor heard the racket and opened the door, he just took one look and went straight to get the principal. He said there had been some terrible accident and the supply closet was full of bloody people, apparently all cut up and screaming in pain.

By the time the principal got there, Miss Newman had pulled herself together and was herding the little kids down the hall to the washroom, and then the recess bell rang.

So the hall was full of kids, and teachers calling to Miss Newman, 'What happened? What happened?' and the principal telling everyone to 'Move along, move right along. Nothing here to see.' Of course there was plenty to see – the whole thing looked like a big disaster we had just read about in history called The Children's Massacre.

In all the commotion Leroy Herdman just walked into the supply closet, untied his snake and put it in his pocket, and walked out again.

When we got back from recess, the principal and Miss Newman and the janitor and the boys' basketball coach were all crawling around the floor of the supply closet, and Miss Newman was saying, 'I tell you there was a snake crawling up the light cord!'

Of course they never did find it, because nobody looked in Leroy's pocket.

I couldn't understand why the snake died and Leroy didn't, but when I asked my father, he said that Leroy probably stretched his story. 'A snake bit him,' my father said, 'and then he found a different snake that was already dead. That's what I think.'

My mother said she bet it wasn't a snake at all, that Leroy just tied a whole lot of poor worms together. But I decided that Leroy was telling the truth for the first time in his life, that the snake was perfectly healthy, bit Leroy, and immediately died. So maybe Mrs. Wendleken wasn't far wrong to pour iodine all over Alice, and maybe Alice should shut up about this treatment and just be glad she wasn't dead, like the snake.

Two or three days later Leroy stuck the snake in the third-grade pencil sharpener, tail first, and that teacher went all to pieces too. It was bad enough, she said, to find a snake in the pencil sharpener, but then she almost sharpened it by mistake.

The snake was pretty worn out by then, so they threw it away, but nobody in the third grade would go near the pencil sharpener for the rest of the week.

My mother's friend Miss Philips worked for the welfare department, and one of her jobs was to check up on the Herdmans, so Mother told her about the snakebite in case Leroy should get some kind of shot for it. But Miss Philips just said she didn't know of any shot that would benefit Leroy, and anyway, all her sympathies were with the snake.

'I went once to that garage where those kids live,' she said, 'but I never got inside and I barely got out of the yard alive. It was full of rocks and poison ivy and torn-up bicycles and pieces of cars and great big holes they'd dug. I fell in one of the holes and the cat jumped on me out of a window. Good thing I had a hat on or I'd be bald. Now I just drive past the place once a month, and if they haven't managed to blow it up or burn it down, I figure they're all right.'

'But a snakebite,' Mother said. 'Don't you think that's unusual?'

'I certainly do,' Miss Philips said. 'It's the first time something bit one of them instead of the other way around.'

The whole thing got into the newspaper: 'REPTILE FOUND IN WOODROW WILSON SCHOOL', the article said. 'TEACHERS AND STUDENTS ALARMED'. That probably meant Miss Newman and all the kindergarten kids. 'PARENTS SEEK ACTION' probably meant Mrs. Wendleken, seeking to get the Herdmans expelled or arrested or something. 'SCHOOL OFFICIAL INSPECTS PREMIES' *was* Mr. Crabtree, the principal, who stuck his head in the third-grade room and said that if one more snake showed up anywhere he would personally kill it, skin it, cook it, and feed it to whoever was responsible.

I don't know whether that would have scared Leroy or not, but it didn't matter anyway because he wasn't there. Imogene said he stayed home to bury the snake, and she had this messy scribbled-up note that said, 'Leroy is absent at a funeral'.

'I'm sorry to hear that, Imogene,' the teacher said. 'Was it a member of your family? Why aren't you at the funeral?'

'It was a friend of Leroy's,' Imogene said. 'I didn't like him.'

Mrs. Wendleken was mad because the newspaper article didn't say it was Leroy. Herdman's snake that caused all this trouble, and she was mad at the principal because he wouldn't say so either.

'I can't *prove* who the snake belonged to,' Mr. Crabtree said, 'and even if I could, why would I? It wasn't a boa constrictor, you know, and it was dead to begin with.'

But I guess Mrs. Wendleken was really out to nail Leroy, and she wouldn't give up. 'Of course it was Leroy's snake! Everybody knows it was Leroy's snake. Why else would he bury it? Why would Leroy Herdman bury someone else's snake?'

'I don't know.' Mr. Crabtree was fed up with the snake and Leroy Herdman and Mrs. Wendleken too. 'But if he *did* bury a snake for somebody else, it's the first cooperative thing he's ever done in his life, and I just think we ought to drop the whole subject, don't you?'

That would probably have been the end of it, except that Mrs. Wendleken described this conversation to my mother, who described it to Miss Philips. Then Miss Philips went to school and told Mr. Crabtree that she had a plan to civilize the Herdmans or, at least, one of them.

'It's about the snake . . .' she began, but Mr. Crabtree wouldn't let her say any more.

'I'll do it,' he said. 'I don't even care what it is you want, just so I don't have to hear any more about that snake.'

So Leroy got named Good School Citizen of the Month – 'for an act of kindness', the award read.

Of course this was one big surprise to everybody, especially Leroy, and it nearly killed Alice Wendleken, who had piled up more good deeds and good grades and extra-credit projects and perfect-attend-ance records than anybody else in the whole history of the Woodrow Wilson School, and expected to be the Good School Citizen of the Month for the rest of her life.

Nobody could figure out what kind thing Leroy had done, but Miss Philips told my mother.

'He buried a snake?' Mother said. 'That's it?'

'That's it,' Miss Philips said.

'Well, I guess if you were the snake you might call it an act of kindness, but I don't understand . . .'

'I just thought he might decide to live up to the honour,' Miss Philips explained. 'He might be a changed person.'

Mother said she wouldn't count on it. 'He prob-ably doesn't even know what it was he did.'

'He didn't even do it,' Charlie told her. 'Imogene just said he did. Nobody buried the snake. The janitor threw it in the trash masher. I saw him.'

'Well, don't tell anyone,' Mother said. 'Mrs. Wen-dleken would never shut up about it.'

Mother was right about Leroy. He *didn't* know what he did or how he got to be a Good School Citizen, and when Charlie wouldn't tell him, he buried Charlie up to his neck in the trash masher barrel, which would have been tough on Charlie if the janitor didn't happen to see him before he mashed up the trash.

So Leroy wasn't a changed person, unless you want to count that he only buried Charlie up to his neck instead of all the way.

CHAPTER FOUR

The janitor, Mr. Sprague, said that was that – no more trash masher. He told the principal that we could have a trash masher or we could have the Herdmans, but we couldn't have both under one roof.

'I can't stand around and guard the thing all day,' he said. 'There's six of them and only one of me, and every time I leave the basement to go sweep a floor, they shove something else into it.'

They'd already mashed up the fourth-grade ant farm and the plastic dinosaur exhibit, and then Leroy went ahead and mashed up the Good School Citizen Award too, once he found out he couldn't eat it or spend it or sell it to anybody.

Alice reported this to her mother, and Mrs. Wendleken was so disgusted about the whole thing that she resigned from the PTA, which my father said was good news for the PTA.

Of course, Mrs. Wendleken didn't come right out and say, 'I quit because I'm mad at everybody.' She just said it wasn't fair for her to run the PTA Talent Show because Alice was in it. She said Mother could do that because Mother *didn't* have any talented children in it.

'Does that mean we aren't talented, or just that we aren't in it?' Charlie asked me, and I said, 'Both.'

Actually *nobody* had any talented children in it, and they really had to scratch around to get kids to do anything, so it was no night of a thousand stars, which was what all the posters said – 'Night of a Thousand Stars! An Evening of Family Entertainment! PTA Talent Show!'

When my father saw the list of acts, he said he hoped there would be more talent in the refreshments than there was going to be in the show.

'There aren't any refreshments,' Mother told him. 'This is just an evening of family entertainment.'

He shook his head. 'Not unless you have refreshments, it won't be.'

I guess Mother took another look at the list, because that night she called around for people to make cookies and brownies and cupcakes and punch, and the next day the posters said, 'Night of a Thousand Stars! An Evening of Family Entertainment! PTA Talent Show!' – with 'Delicious Refreshments!' crowded in at the bottom.

This was a big mistake, because 'refreshments' is one long word that all the Herdmans understand, and right away you knew that they'd figure some way to get at them.

'They can't,' Alice said. 'They'd have to be in the show, and they can't do anything talented.'

'They can steal,' Charlie said.

Alice looked at him the way my mother looks at the bottom of the hamster cage. 'That's not a talent,' she said.

Maybe not, but the Herdmans did it better than anybody else. Still, it was hard to see how they would do it for an audience or what they would call it on the programme or what they would steal, because there wasn't much left that they hadn't already stolen.

Last year they were all absent on October 4 and we had Arbor Day because for the last three years the Herdmans stole the tree, and the principal said at least this year we'd finally get it planted, even if it died over the winter.

'Maybe they've got some talent we don't know about,' I said. And sure enough, three days later Gladys Herdman took a pair of kindergarten safety scissors and cut Eugene Preston's hair in the shape of a dog. It could have been a cat, though, or a horse or a pig. Something with four legs and a tail, anyway, or else something with five legs and no tail.

You had to look right down at the top of his head to see it, but this was what you mostly saw of Eugene anyway because he was the shortest kid in the second grade or the first grade or even kindergarten. So naturally he got picked on a lot, and if you had to choose which kid in the Woodrow Wilson School would get his hair cut in the shape of a dog for no reason, you would choose Eugene.

Of course he was already a nervous wreck from being the shortest kid around, and you knew it wasn't going to calm him down to have people holler, 'Here, Fido!' or 'Here, Spot!' at him. And if his hair was anything like the rest of him, he would probably be this way for years. So things didn't look good for Eugene.

'A dog?' my father said when he heard about it. 'I can't believe it looks like a dog. Who says it looks like a dog?'

'The art teacher,' Charlie said. 'I heard her tell the principal. She said if it just wasn't on Eugene's head she would display it as an example of living sculpture.'

'Why don't you tell that to Eugene?' Mother said. 'It might make him feel better to know that he's a living sculpture.'

I didn't think so. For one thing, nobody knew what a living sculpture was. I helped Eugene look it up in the encyclopedia, but we looked under *living* instead of *sculpture* and never got past *living sacrifice*, which was all about torture, and *that* sure didn't make Eugene feel better.

'Come on, Eugene,' I said. 'Don't be crazy. No one's going to make you be a sacrifice.'

'Hah!' he said. 'How about Gladys Herdman?'

He was really worried, and between being worried and short and having his hair all chopped up, Eugene began to twitch and wiggle and bite his fingernails and bang himself on the head.

'I can't help it,' he said. 'It makes me feel better.'

Actually, there wasn't a kid in the Woodrow Wilson School who didn't wiggle or twitch or tie knots in his hair or *something*. Boomer Malone once ate a whole pencil without even knowing it till he

106

got to the eraser and broke off a tooth. Some kids banged their heads, too, when they didn't have anything else to do, and of course the Herdmans banged *other* kids on the head, but nobody did it as hard as Eugene.

This was fascinating to Gladys Herdman. She quit hitting him and hollering at him and just followed him around everywhere – waiting for him to knock himself out, we all thought.

'Why do you do that all the time?' she asked him, but Eugene was scared to tell her the truth. He figured if he said, 'It makes me feel better', she would pound him black and blue and claim it was a good deed.

My mother thought Eugene ought to enter the talent show. 'It would take his mind off his troubles,' she said, 'and there must be *something* he could do.'

I couldn't imagine what, except maybe stand up on the stage and be short, and I never heard of a show where part of the entertainment was somebody being short. So I was pretty surprised, along with everybody else, to learn that Eugene had a hidden talent that he would perform at the talent show.

'And then on TV, probably,' Gladys Herdman said. Gladys was the one who discovered this talent but she wouldn't tell anybody what it was and she wouldn't let Eugene tell anybody either, not even his mother – so Mrs. Preston didn't know whether to get him a costume or a guitar or elevator shoes or what.

My mother didn't know what to put on the stage

for him to use. 'Maybe he needs a microphone,' she said. 'Maybe he needs some special music. I'd really like to know, because I want Eugene to be a success.' It would be wonderful, she told us, if Eugene could win first prize in the talent show.

What she really meant was, it would be wonderful if *anybody* besides Alice Wendleken would win first prize for a change, but I knew that wouldn't happen unless Alice broke both her arms and couldn't play the piano.

I guess Charlie thought it was worth a try, though, because he asked Eugene what he needed for his talent act.

'He needs walnuts,' Charlie reported, 'but he says he'll bring his own. He doesn't want to. He's scared to be in the talent show, but he's more scared of Gladys.'

'What's he going to do with walnuts?' Mother asked.

'I don't know. Unless . . . maybe he's going to juggle them.' Charlie brightened up. 'That would be good! Even if he drops some, that would be good!'

It seemed to me that if Eugene could juggle *any-thing* we would all know about it, but maybe not. My friend Betty Lou Sampson is double-jointed and can fold herself into a pretzel, but she won't do it in front of people, because of being shy. It could be the same way with Eugene, I thought.

I also thought he might back out, but on the night of the talent show there he was, so for once we had something different to look forward to.

There isn't usually anything different or surprising about the talent show. One year a girl named Bernice Potts signed up to do an animal act and the animal turned out to be a goldfish, which was different. But then the act turned out to be Bernice talking to the fish and the fish talking back and Bernice telling the audience what the fish said. Charlie loved this, but he was in the first grade then and believed anything anybody told him.

Mrs. Wendleken said this act didn't belong in the talent show because it didn't have anything to do with human talent. 'Even if the fish *could* talk,' she said, 'that would just mean the fish was talented, not Bernice.'

Mrs. Wendleken didn't think Eugene should be juggling walnuts either, according to Alice. '*If* he can do it,' Alice sniffed, 'which he probably can't.'

Eugene didn't even try. He came out on the stage carrying a big bowl of walnuts while Mother was introducing him. 'Our next talented performer,' she said, 'is from the second grade. It's Eugene Preston, and Eugene is going to – '

Mother never got a chance to finish, because Eugene began smashing walnuts on his forehead one after another, just as fast as he could, and walnut shells flew everywhere.

People sitting in the back of the auditorium couldn't figure out what he was doing, and people sitting in the front of the auditorium knew what he was doing but couldn't believe he was doing it. The principal, who was sitting in the back row, thought kids were throwing things at Eugene, so he started up the aisle and ran smack into Mrs. Preston, who was yelling for someone to stop Eugene before he killed himself with walnuts.

Nobody heard her. There was too much noise. Kids were jumping up and down and clapping and hollering, 'Go, Eugene! Go, Eugene!' and then, 'Go, Hammerhead! Go, Hammerhead!' Boomer Malone began counting walnuts: ' . . . twenty-two, twenty-three, twenty-four . . .' And pretty soon everybody was chanting, ' . . . thirty-six, thirty-seven, thirty-eight . . .' Boomer said Mrs. Preston fainted when Eugene got to forty-five walnuts, but she didn't really faint. She just collapsed on to a seat, moaning something about 'scrambled brains'.

Eugene used all his walnuts and then he set his bowl down on the stage and walked off. He looked taller to me, but that's probably because I was looking up at him for a change.

Eugene didn't win first prize, but neither did Alice. Her piano solo was called 'Flying Fingers', and it would have been pretty flashy except that there were so many walnut shells stuck in the piano keys that she kept having to stop and start over. Eugene was the popular favourite, but I guess the judges didn't want to reward a scramble-your-brains act, in case that *did* eventually happen to him, so they gave the first prize to the kindergarten rhythm band, which was probably the best thing to do. It made all the kindergarten mothers happy and it didn't make anyone else very mad.

Of course, kids were all over Eugene, telling him that he should have won, that he was the best, and wanting to feel his head.

'Did you always crack nuts that way?' someone asked, and Eugene said no, that it was Gladys Herdman's idea.

'Why?' Charlie said. 'What was in it for Gladys?'

If you didn't know any better you might think that Gladys felt guilty because of Eugene's dog haircut, but no one at the Woodrow Wilson School would think that. So when we went to get the delicious refreshments, no one was very surprised to find they were all gone.

Mrs. McCluskey was in charge of the food, and when Mother asked her what happened she said, 'I'd just put the last plate of cupcakes on the table when Gladys Herdman ran in here yelling that Eugene Preston had gone crazy in the auditorium and was trying to kill himself. Now normally I wouldn't pay any attention to *anything* a Herdman told me, but I could hear a lot of noise and stamping around and people yelling, 'Eugene! Eugene!', so naturally I went to see.' She shrugged. 'I still don't know what happened to Eugene, but I know what happened to the refreshments.'

Everybody knew what happened to the refreshments but as usual you couldn't prove anything because the evidence was gone and Gladys was gone.

Mrs. Wendleken didn't agree. She said the evidence was Eugene. 'It's obvious that Gladys Herdman got that poor little boy to knock himself

111

silly and cause a big commotion, and then she went to the cafeteria and walked off with every last cookie!'

Maybe so, but Eugene *didn't* knock himself silly and you couldn't feel very sorry for him because he was a big celebrity with his name in the newspaper – 'Unusual Performance by Plucky Eugene Preston Earns Standing Ovation at Woodrow Wilson Talent Show'. The article also mentioned the kindergarten rhythm band, but not by name ('Too many of them,' the reporter said) and not by musical number ('Could have been almost anything').

Besides, Eugene wasn't even Eugene anymore except to his mother and the teachers. And sometimes even the teachers forgot and called him Hammerhead, just like everyone else.

CHAPTER FIVE

Every now and then I would remember about the assignment for the year – Compliments for Class-mates – and turn to that page in my notebook. So far I had thought up compliments for six people, including Alice. For Alice, I put down 'Important'.

'I'm not sure I'd call that a compliment,' my mother said.

'Alice would,' I told her. Actually, Alice would probably consider it just a natural fact, like 'The earth is round', 'The sky is blue', 'Alice Wendleken is important'.

Alice began being important right away in the first grade because she was the only first-grade kid who had ever been inside the teachers' room. So when-ever something had to be delivered there, Alice got to deliver it.

'I have a note to go to the teachers' room,' our teacher would say, 'way up on the third floor, so Alice, I'll ask you to be my messenger since you know exactly where it is.'

Then Alice would stand up and straighten her dress and pat her hair and carry the note in both hands out in front of her as if it was news from God.

Most of all, she would never tell what was in the room.

Whenever the teachers didn't have anything else to do, they went and hid in the teachers' room, but nobody else ever got in there. You couldn't *see* in, either, because the door was wood and frosted glass almost to the top.

Boomer Malone once got Charlie to climb on his shoulders and look in, but all Charlie could see was a sign that said 'Thank God It's Friday', and another sign that said 'Thank God It's June'.

This got spread around school, and kids went home and told about the swear words in the teachers' room, so after that they put up a curtain and nobody could see anything.

'There isn't anything to see,' my mother said. 'Just some chairs and tables and a sofa and a big coffeepot and a little refrigerator.'

'No TV?' Charlie said.

'No TV.'

'What do they do in there?'

Mother sighed. 'I suppose they relax,' she said, 'and talk to each other, and have lunch.'

'That's not what Imogene Herdman says,' Charlie muttered.

'Well,' Mother said, 'if you believe what Imogene Herdman says, you'll believe anything.'

'They go in there to smoke cigarettes and drink Cokes' was what Imogene had said. 'And if some-body has a cake, they put it in a Sears, Roebuck sack and pretend it's something they bought, and then they go in there and eat it where nobody can see them. And they don't let anybody in who doesn't know the password.'

Charlie brightened right up. 'What's the password?'

'They pick a new one every day,' Imogene said, 'and then they put it in the morning announcements, like in what's for lunch. Once it was *macaroni and cheese.*'

I figured Imogene was making this up as she went along, so you had to be impressed with her imagination. I even got out my notebook and started to write that down: Imogene Herdman – 'Has imagination'. But then I realized it wasn't imagination, it was just a big lie. I also realized that finding a compliment for Imogene Herdman was probably the hardest thing I'd have to do all year and I'd better start thinking about it.

Of course, Charlie kept waiting for *macaroni and cheese* to show up in the morning announcements. He was going to walk past the teachers' room and say 'macaroni and cheese' and see what happened. But the next time it was on the lunch menu, Charlie was stuck in the nurse's room with a nosebleed and didn't get to try it.

Imogene told him it didn't make any difference because the password that day was *softball.*

'Did you try it?' Charlie asked. 'Did you get in?'

'I don't want in.' Imogene gave him this dark, squinty-eyed look. 'If a kid gets in that room, they never let him out. Remember Pauline Ellison?'

Charlie shook his head.

'Neither does anyone else. She got in the teachers' room. Remember Kenneth Weaver? Did you see Kenneth Weaver lately?'

'No, because he's got the mumps.'

'That's what you think. Kenneth doesn't have the mumps. Kenneth got caught in the teachers' room.'

I guess this was too much, even for Charlie. 'I don't believe you,' he said.

Imogene grinned her girl-Godzilla grin. 'Neither did Kenneth,' she said. 'I told him he better not go near the teachers' room but' – she shrugged – 'he did it anyway.'

For once nobody believed Imogene. Nobody *told* her so, but Alice Wendleken said that from now on Imogene couldn't shove people around anymore because she was a proven liar, and no matter what she said everybody would laugh at her and maybe knock her down. Nobody believed *that* either, but it sounded great.

'Just wait till Kenneth comes back!' everybody said. But Kenneth didn't come back.

Charlie hunted me up at recess with this news. 'He's never coming back,' he said. 'The teacher gathered up his books and moved Bernadette Slocum into his seat and said, "Well, we'll certainly miss Kenneth, won't we?" It's just like Imogene said!'

'Oh, come on, Charlie,' I said. 'You know they haven't got him shut up in the teachers' room.'

Still . . . you had to wonder. First Imogene said

116

Kenneth was gone, and then he *was* gone. What if Imogene was right?

I wasn't the only one who thought about this, and I wasn't the only one who found reasons to stay away from the teachers' room, and even to stay away from the whole third floor. Kids suddenly couldn't climb stairs for one reason or another or kids got dizzy if they went above the second floor. Alice had what she called a twisted toe and limped around holding on to chairs and tables, all on one floor, naturally.

But Louella McCluskey told the real truth, for everyone. 'I don't *think* Imogene Herdman is right,' she said, 'and I don't *think* kids disappear into the teachers' room, but maybe she is and maybe they do, and I'm not going to take any chances.'

Then two teachers and a district supervisor and Mrs. Wendleken all got locked in the teachers' room by accident. They were in there for an hour and a half, banging on the door and yelling and even throwing things out the window. They took down the curtain and climbed up on chairs and waved their arms around at the top of the door, but nobody saw them and nobody heard them because nobody ever went near the teachers' room.

They were all pretty mad, especially the district supervisor, and Mrs. Wendleken was hysterical by the time somebody let them out. By that time, too, they were all worn out and hoarse from yelling and dizzy from waving their arms around in the air.

Who finally let them out was Imogene.

She said that she stood around trying to decide

what to do, and that made Mrs. Wendleken hysterical all over again. 'What to do!' she said. 'Open the door and let us out is what to do!'

'But it's the teachers' room,' Imogene said, looking shocked, as if she had this rule burned into her brain. 'We're not allowed in the teachers' room.'

'You're allowed to let people *out* of the teachers' room!' Mrs. Wendleken hollered.

Then the district supervisor got mad at Mrs. Wendleken. 'This child has saved the day,' she said. 'We ought to thank her. And let me tell you, there are plenty of schools in this district where the students spend every waking minute trying to break into the teachers' room, or sneak into the teachers' room. You wouldn't believe the wild tales I've heard. Now here's a student who seems to understand that teachers need a little privacy. I hope you have more boys and girls like . . . is it Imogene?'

'We have five more exactly like her,' one of the teachers said.

The district supervisor said that was wonderful and nobody argued with her – too tired, I guess, from jumping up and down and yelling for help.

This whole thing got in the newspaper. 'SCHOOL PERSONNEL LOCKED IN THIRD FLOOR ROOM', it said. 'RELEASED BY ALERT STUDENT'. It didn't name the alert student but it named everybody else who was there.

'Except Kenneth Weaver,' Charlie said. 'It doesn't say anything about Kenneth Weaver.'

'That proves it, Charlie,' I said. 'He never was in there.'

'Why in the world would Kenneth Weaver be in the teachers' room?' Mother said. 'That whole family moved to Toledo.'

'Did they take Kenneth?' Charlie asked.

'Certainly they took Kenneth! Who would move away and leave their children?'

'Mr. Herdman,' I said, but Mother said that was different.

Alice Wendleken cut out the newspaper article and gave it to Imogene. 'I thought you'd want to keep it,' she said, 'since it's about you. Of course nobody knows it's about you because they didn't print your name. I wonder why they didn't print your name.'

'They didn't print Kenneth's name either,' Imogene said. 'So what?'

'So Kenneth wasn't there!' Alice said.

Imogene stuck her nose right up against Alice's nose, which naturally made Alice nervous and also cross-eyed. 'Why do you think I opened the door to that room?' she said. 'You think I opened the door to let all those teachers out? Who cares if they never get out? I let Kenneth out.'

'My mother was in there,' Alice said, 'and she didn't see Kenneth.'

'Did you ask her?'

'No, because I know Kenneth Weaver is in Toledo.'

'He is now,' Imogene said.

119

This was typical Herdman – too shifty to figure out, and Alice didn't even try.

Aside from congratulating Imogene, the district supervisor said that the worst part of being shut up in there for an hour and a half was the furniture. 'Lumpy old sofa,' she said, 'broken-down chairs, terrible lighting. It doesn't surprise me that the door was broken. Everything in that room is broken.'

So the teachers got a new sofa and chairs, and the furniture store donated a new rug, and they painted the walls and fixed the door and bought new curtains and a big green plant.

They left the door open too for a couple of days so everybody could see the new stuff, which just went to prove, Alice said, 'that there's nobody hidden there and never was'.

Imogene shrugged. 'Suit yourself.'

Charlie was feeling brave too. 'Where would they be?' he said. 'There's no place for them.'

'Sure there is.' Imogene pointed. 'How about that? The plant that ate Chicago.'

'The plant?' Mother said that evening. 'Well, I would have chosen some normal kind of plant like a fern, but I guess they wanted something scientific for the teachers' room. That plant is a Venus fly-trap. It eats flies . . . swallows them right up.'

Charlie looked at me, his eyes wide, and I knew what he was thinking – that maybe you could say the password by accident, disappear into the teachers' room, and never be seen again because of death by plant.

'It eats *flies*, Charlie,' I said. 'Nothing but flies.'

'Well, after all, it's just a plant,' Mother said. 'It doesn't know flies from hamburger. I guess it eats anything it can get hold of.'

Once Charlie spread the word around, you would normally have had kids lining up to feed stuff to the plant – pizza, potato chips, M&M cookies – and they would probably have had to keep the door locked and put up a big sign that said 'Private, Keep Out, Teachers Only'. But none of this happened because nobody would go near the teachers' room, not even to watch a plant eat lunch.

When the district supervisor came back to see the new furniture, she mentioned this and said that the teachers could thank 'that thoughtful girl. What was her name? Imogene' for all this peace and privacy.

I guess she was right, in a way, but I didn't see any teachers rushing to thank Imogene. And never mind how much I needed to find a compliment for her, I certainly couldn't write down 'Imogene Herdman is thoughtful', no matter what the district supervisor said.

CHAPTER SIX

Once a year we had to take an IQ test and a psychology test and an aptitude test, which showed what you might grow up to be if the Herdmans let you get out of the Woodrow Wilson School alive. But the only test the Herdmans ever bothered to take was the eye test.

This surprised everybody, because it meant that at least they knew the letters of the alphabet. You had to cover up one eye with a little piece of paper and read the letters on a chart, and then cover up the other eye and read them again. If you couldn't do it, it meant that you had to have glasses.

Sometimes it just meant that you were scared, like Lester Yeagle.

'If you don't do it right,' Gladys Herdman told Lester, 'it means your eyes are in backward, and they have to take them out and put them in the other way.'

This made Lester so nervous that he couldn't tell *L* from *M* or *X* from *K*, and when the doctor said, 'Well, let's just switch eyes,' he went all to pieces and had to go lie down in the nurse's room till his mother could come and get him.

Besides having three other kids and a baby, Mrs.

Yeagle was a schoolbus driver, so she couldn't waste much time just letting Lester be hysterical. But Lester was too hysterical to tell her what happened – all he said was 'Herdman.'

'Which one?' Mrs. Yeagle said. 'Which one did it?' and Lester said Gladys did it.

'Did what?' the nurse wanted to know. 'Gladys wasn't even there.'

'I don't know what,' Mrs. Yeagle said, 'and I can't wait around to find out because I had to leave the baby with the Avon lady and it's almost time to drive the bus. Come on, Lester, honey . . . maybe you can find out,' she told the nurse.

Of course Gladys said she didn't do anything, and the eye doctor said *he* certainly didn't do anything. 'But I got a look at that kid's braces,' he said, 'and I'll bet that's his problem.'

I didn't think so. Having braces was no problem – *not* having braces was a problem. Gloria Coburn's little sister got braces and Gloria didn't, and Gloria cried and carried on for weeks. 'I'll grow up ugly with an overbite,' she said, and she didn't even know for sure what one was. She just wanted braces like everyone else.

That night the nurse called Mrs. Yeagle to say that apparently Gladys didn't do anything to Lester. 'We think the trouble may be his braces,' she suggested.

'What braces?' Mrs. Yeagle said. 'Lester doesn't have braces.' But then she went and looked in his mouth and she nearly died.

'What have you got in there?' she yelled. 'What is all that? It looks like paper clips!'

Sure enough, Lester had paper clips bent around his teeth and he got hysterical all over again because his mother pried them off.

The nurse said she never heard of paper clips, 'but you know they all want to have braces or bands or something. And they don't know how much braces cost.'

'Well, these cost thirty-five cents,' Mrs. Yeagle said. 'According to Lester, Gladys Herdman put them on him and that's what she charged him. And let me tell you, that kid better never try to get on my bus! Or any other Herdmans either!'

Getting thrown off the bus was almost the worst thing that could happen to you. You had to go to school anyway, no matter what, so if you got thrown off the bus it meant that your father had to hang around and take you, or your mother had to stop whatever she was doing and take you, so you got yelled at right and left. You even got yelled at when it happened to someone else – 'Don't *you* get thrown off the bus!' your mother would say.

Mrs. Herdman probably never said this, but she didn't have to worry about it anyway. The Herdmans never got thrown off a bus because nobody ever let them on one. Sometimes, though, they would hang around what would have been their bus stop if they had one, smoking cigars and starting fights and telling little kids that the bus was full of bugs.

'Big bugs,' Gladys told Maxine Cooper's little

brother, Donald. 'Didn't you ever hear them? They chomp through anything to get food. You better give me your lunch, Donald. I'll take it to school for you.'

Of course that was the end of Donald's lunch, but at least, Maxine said, it was just a day-old bologna sandwich and some carrot sticks so they probably wouldn't do that again.

'They're just jealous,' Alice told her, 'because they have to walk while everybody else gets to ride and be warm and comfortable.'

'Come on, Alice,' I said. 'If you think the schoolbus is warm and comfortable, you must be out of your mind.'

But Imogene Herdman was standing right behind us, so Alice ignored me and said again how wonderful it was to ride the schoolbus, and how she would hate to be the Herdmans who *couldn't* ride the schoolbus because they were so awful.

After that they began to show up every morning at Maxine's bus stop, looking sneaky and dangerous, like some outlaw gang about to hold up the stagecoach.

'But they don't do anything,' Maxine said, looking worried. 'They just stand around. It's scary.'

It scared Donald, all right, and after three or four days he wouldn't even come out the door, so Maxine stood on her front porch and yelled, 'My mother says for you to go home!'

'We can't go home!' Imogene yelled back. 'We have to go to school.'

Then they all nodded at each other, Maxine said,

just as if they were this big normal family of ordinary kids who got up and brushed their teeth and combed their hair and marched out ready to learn something.

Maxine felt pretty safe on her own porch, so she said, 'Then why don't you just get on the bus and go!'

'Get on *your* bus?' Imogene said. 'Get on Bus Six?' And Gladys hollered that she wouldn't get on Bus 6 if it was the last bus in the world, and Leroy said, 'Me neither.'

'And then when the bus came,' Maxine told us, 'they all ran behind the McCarthys' front hedge and just stood there, staring at us.'

'What did Mrs. Yeagle do?' I asked.

'She yelled at them, "Don't you kids even think about getting on my bus!" and Ollie said, "I'll never get on Bus Six!" He said it twice. Listen . . .' Maxine leaned forward and lowered her voice. 'I think the Herdmans are scared of the bus.'

This was the craziest thing I'd ever heard. 'It's just a bus,' I said.

'I *know* that,' Maxine said, 'but it's my bus and I have to ride on it, and I don't want to ride on a doomed bus!'

This sounded crazy too, but nobody laughed, because if the Herdmans *were* scared of Bus 6, it was the *only* thing in the world they were scared of, so you had to figure they must know something no one else knew.

Whatever it was, they weren't telling, but every

day there they were at the bus stop, whispering and shaking their heads.

Charlie thought they were stealing pieces of the bus, one little piece at a time, and someday the whole bus would just fall apart and scatter kids all over the street.

Eugene Preston brought in a copy of *Amazing Comics*, about a robot bus that suddenly began to go backward and sideways and turn itself over and lock all its doors, so the people were trapped inside, yelling and screaming. In the comic book the Mighty Marvo showed up and rescued everybody, but Eugene said he wouldn't want to count on the Mighty Marvo if he was up against the Herdmans.

'I just know something's going to happen,' Maxine said. 'I keep hearing this strange noise on the bus.'

I don't know how she would hear anything except kids hollering, but Eloise Albright said she heard a strange noise too. Some kids said they smelled something on the bus, but who doesn't? – egg sandwiches, poison ivy medicine, Alice Wendleken's Little Princess perfume.

Lester finally asked his mother if there was anything wrong with their bus, but she just said, 'Yes, it's full of kids.'

Then Bus 6 was assigned to take the third grade to a dairy farm to study cows, and Ollie Herdman refused to go. 'Not me,' Ollie said. 'Not on *that* bus!'

Of course this was good news for the cows, and the teacher was pretty happy, but the rest of the third grade was scared to death. Boomer Malone's little sister Gwenda said the suspense was awful – waiting for the bus to blow up or turn over – and between that and having to milk a cow, the whole third grade was wiped out for the rest of the day.

By this time Maxine was a nervous wreck, along with Donald and Lester and everybody else on Bus 6. More and more kids were feeling sick to their stomachs and then feeling fine as soon as the bus left, and they all said the same thing – that they were scared to ride the bus because the Herdmans wouldn't get on it.

'What kind of reason is that?' my mother wanted to know. 'Of course they won't get on the bus. Thelma Yeagle won't *let* them on the bus. Nobody *wants* them on the bus!'

'Something bad is going to happen,' Charlie told her, 'and the Herdmans know what it is. That's why they won't get on. They know Bus Six is doomed.'

'Doomed!' Mother stared at him. 'You watch too much television. Is that what everybody thinks?'

We said yes.

'Then why doesn't somebody just put the Herdmans on the bus and make them ride it?' Mother said.

Since it wasn't my bus, I thought that was a good idea and so did Charlie and so did Mr. Crabtree, I guess, because that's what he did.

'We have to ride your bus, Lester,' Gladys said. She grinned this big grin so Lester could see her teeth all shiny with paper clips. 'The principal said.'

'I thought you were scared to ride this bus,' Maxine told Imogene. 'You said it was doomed.'

'I didn't say that,' Imogene told her. '*You* said that.' She climbed on the bus and walked up and down the aisle, picking out a seat next to some victim. 'It looks all right to me.'

Mrs. Yeagle was pretty mad at first, but she told my mother it wasn't all bad to have the Herdmans on the bus. 'They told everybody to shut up,' she said, 'and everybody did.'

Not for long, though. Claude and Leroy stole a bunch of baby turtles from the pet store and took them on the bus and put them down some kids' shirts. Leroy said later that he was amazed at what happened. He thought the turtles were dead and he was going to take them back to the pet store and complain.

The turtles weren't dead. They probably saw who had them and decided to stay in their shells till they were big enough to bite back. But it was nice and warm inside the shirts, so they began to stick their heads out and crawl around.

Of course nobody knew they had turtles down their backs. Nobody knew *what* they had down their backs, but Donald Cooper thought it was the big bugs, hungry and tired of peanut butter sandwiches. 'I've got the big bugs on me!' he yelled, and right away all the other kids began to yell and scream and jump up and down and thrash around so Mrs. Yeagle had to stop the bus and get everybody settled down.

It was another week before all the turtles came out

from under the seats and behind the seat backs so it was a good thing that they were little to begin with and didn't grow very fast.

Once the Herdmans had collected all the turtles, they got off the bus and never came back. 'Don't want to ride this dumb bus,' Ralph muttered, and I guess that was the real truth. They just wanted to get *on* the bus, take over the territory, wham a few kids, pick out the best lunch (Gwenda Malone's, usually, because Gwenda always had two desserts and no healthy food), and then get *off* the bus and stay off, which they did.

For once, though, they weren't the only ones who got what they wanted. Lester's baby teeth fell out like popcorn – 'All those paper clips,' Mrs. Yeagle said – and his second teeth came in all crooked and side-ways, so he had more braces and bigger braces and fancier braces than anybody else in the Woodrow Wilson School, and maybe the whole world.

CHAPTER SEVEN

When Louella McCluskey's mother went to work part-time at the telephone company, she let Louella baby-sit her little brother, Howard, again during spring vacation.

'Just don't you let the Herdmans get him this time,' she said. 'He's got hair now so they can't draw all over his head but I don't know what else they might do.'

Howard had hair all right, but it was no big improvement because it started way above his ears and grew straight up, like grass.

'If it was up to me,' Louella said, 'I'd shave his head and let him start all over.'

'Just mention that to Leroy,' I said.

Louella turned pale. 'My mother would kill me, and I'd never get to watch television or go to the movies for the rest of my life.'

Louella kept Howard out of sight for the whole time, but when school started again, the regular baby-sitter quit, so Mrs. McCluskey got special permission for Louella to bring Howard to school – 'Just for a few days,' she said. 'Just till I find someone else.'

'Now what'll I do?' Louella said. 'I can't learn compound fractions and watch out for Howard all the time, and he'll be right there in the same room with Imogene Herdman!'

She was really worried and you couldn't blame her, so I wasn't too surprised when she showed up with Howard on a leash.

Miss Kemp was pretty surprised, though. 'Is that necessary, Louella?' she asked. 'After all, your little brother is our guest here in the sixth grade. Is that how we want to treat a guest, class?'

Some kids said no, but a lot of kids said yes because they figured Howard was going to be a pain in the neck. So then Miss Kemp spent ten minutes talking about manners and hospitality, but I guess *she* figured Howard might be a pain in the neck too because she didn't make Louella untie him.

She did make her get a longer leash, though, because Howard got knocked on his bottom every time he tried to go somewhere.

'He better learn not to do that,' Imogene Herdman said. 'Claude had to learn not to do that.'

Miss Kemp looked at her. 'Not to do what?'

'Not to go past the end of his leash.

'Why was Claude on a leash?'

'Because we didn't have a dog,' Imogene said.

Miss Kemp frowned and sort of shook her head – the way you do when you've got water in your ears and everything sounds strange and faraway – but she didn't ask to hear any more and you couldn't blame her.

Louella poked me. 'If they wanted a dog,' she said,

'they could just go to the Animal Rescue. That's where we got our dog.'

That might be okay for Louella, but I didn't think the Animal Rescue people would give the Herdmans a rescued goldfish, let alone a whole dog, and the Herdmans probably knew it.

Maybe they even went there and said, 'We want a dog,' and the Animal Rescue said, 'Not on your life.' So then, I guess, they just looked around and said, 'Okay, Claude, you be the dog,' and then Claude was the dog till he got tired of it or they got tired of it.

You had to wonder what he *did* when he was the dog – bite people, maybe, except they had Gladys to do that.

Boomer Malone thought he might bark and guard the house.

'From what?' I asked.

Boomer shrugged. 'I don't know . . . robbers?'

'Boomer, who are the main robbers around here?'

'Oh, yeah.' He nodded. 'They are.'

Kids who *didn't* have dogs thought he might come when somebody called him, or sit up and beg, or roll over, or fetch papers. Kids who *did* have dogs said their dogs barked to get in and barked to get out, and chased cars, and swiped food off the table, and tore up the neighbours' trash, and all those things sounded more like Claude. You could see, though, how he would get tired of it.

'He probably got tired of being on a leash,' Alice said. 'Not like *some* people I know.' She meant Howard. Alice had already told Louella what she thought about Howard. 'I tried to teach your little brother to read,' she'd said, 'so he would be ready for kindergarten like I was. But I don't think they'll even let him *in* kindergarten. He's pretty dumb.'

'He's too little to be dumb,' Louella grumbled. 'If you want to teach him something, you could teach him to go to the bathroom.'

Well, I knew that wouldn't happen because Alice won't even say the word *bathroom*. It's a good thing you can just raise your hand to be excused, because if Alice had to say where she was going she would never go, and I don't know what would happen to her.

Dumb or not, Howard was okay for such a little kid struck in the sixth grade. He had lots of paper and crayons, and little boxes of cereal to eat, and different people brought him different things to play with and look at. Alice showed up with great big pieces of cardboard that said *A* and *B* and *C*, but Howard didn't like those much. He scribbled all over them, which, Alice said, just proved how dumb he was, that he didn't even recognize the alphabet. 'He'll never get into kindergarten,' she said again. To hear Alice, you would think getting into kinder-garten was better than getting into heaven, and a whole lot harder.

'They'll never let him in with *that*!' she said the first time she saw Howard's blanket, and for once you had to think she might be right. Howard's blanket was gross. Louella said it used to be blue and it used to have bunnies on it, but now it just looked like my father's car-washing rag.

'He has to have it,' Louella said. 'If he didn't have his blanket, Miss Kemp would probably have to throw him out. If he doesn't have his blanket, he cries and yells and jumps up and down, and if he still doesn't have his blanket, he holds his breath and turns purple.'

Right away Boomer Malone scooped up the blanket and sat on it, which would have caused a big argument except that everyone *wanted* to see Howard turn purple. It was recess and there was already a bunch of kids gathered around Howard at one end of the playground, and naturally more kids came to see what was going on, and by the time Howard quit hollering and began to hold his breath, half the Woodrow Wilson School was there, trying to see over and around people.

'What's he doing?' I heard someone say. 'Is he purple yet?'

He wasn't, and I didn't think he would *live* to be purple, with his eyes popping and all his little head veins standing out.

'Louella,' I said, 'do something . . . he's going to explode!'

'No, he won't,' she said. 'He never does. You can't explode from holding your breath. It's a scientific fact. He won't even pass out. You'll see.'

I didn't want to see – what if Louella was wrong? – but it didn't matter anyway because all of a sudden Imogene Herdman charged up, shoving kids out of the way right and left, and began to pound on Louella.

'You said he would turn purple!' she said. 'Look at him, he's not purple. I can't stand around here all day waiting for him to turn purple. Here, kid.' She threw Howard his blanket and Howard let out this big loud shuddery sob. Then he went on sobbing and hiccuping and hugging his blanket while Imogene stalked off and the whole big crowd of kids grumbled at Louella as if it was her fault.

'I should just take his blanket away right now,' Louella said, 'and let everybody look at him and that would be that. But as far as I know he never had to hold his breath two times so close together and I don't know what that would do to him.'

I thought it would probably kill him, so I was glad she didn't do it, but I knew plenty of kids *would* do it if they got the chance.

My mother said it better not be me or Charlie if we knew what was good for us. 'That poor child has been scribbled on and scrubbed with scouring powder. He's been bald and shiny-headed and now what hair he's got looks as if someone planted it. Isn't that enough for one little boy?'

Either Imogene agreed with my mother or else she had plans to exhibit Howard at some later date ('See the Amazing Purple Baby! 25 cents') and didn't want him used up. From then on she kept one eye on Howard and the other eye on his blanket, and when Wesley Potter tried to snatch Howard's blanket, he never knew what hit him.

Imogene smacked Wesley flat and then stood him up and *held* him up by the ears and said, 'You leave that blanket alone and you leave that kid alone or I'll wrap your whole head in chewing gum so tight they'll have to peel it off along with all your hair and your eyebrows and your lip skin and everything!'

That took care of Wesley and everybody else who heard it, but it made Louella nervous.

'Why is she being nice to Howard?' Louella said. 'Why did she get his blanket back? That's twice she's gotten Howard's blanket back. Why?'

I didn't know why but I knew she wouldn't have to do it again because nobody wants to go through life wrapped in gum *or* skinned bald, and that would be your choice.

'Maybe she likes him,' I said.

'Why would she like him?' Louella said. 'I don't even like him and he's my own brother.'

'But that's normal,' I said. 'I'm not crazy about Charlie either. If Howard was somebody else's brother you'd like him. *I* like him. There's nothing not to like unless he *is* your brother and you have to bring him to school and watch out for him and keep him on a leash and all.'

'Keep him on a leash . . .' Louella repeated. 'Remember what Imogene said? They kept Claude on a leash because they didn't have a dog?'

'So?'

'Well, they still don't have a dog, and here's Howard already on a leash . . . O-o-h!' Louella

137

squealed. 'Imogene is going to make him be their dog and my mother will kill me!'

'Come on, Louella,' I said. 'You can't make a person be a dog. They could *pretend* Howard is their dog, but . . .'

'Just look at Howard,' Louella said. 'He'll pretend anything Imogene wants him to.'

This was true. Howard was hugging his blanket and feeling his one favourite corner (which was even rattier than the whole rest of the blanket) and looking at Imogene the way you would look at the tooth fairy, handing out ten dollars a tooth.

'She'll feed him dog biscuits and teach him to bite!' Louella moaned.

'Maybe he'll bite Gladys,' I said, 'and there's nothing wrong with dog biscuits. Everybody eats dog biscuits at least once to see what they taste like.'

I personally didn't care for them, but when Charlie was little he was crazy about this one brand called Puppy Pleasers. I once asked him how they tasted and he knew exactly.

'If you take a chocolate bar to the beach,' he said, 'and put it in the sand and let it melt and then pick up the melted chocolate bar and the sand and stick it all in the freezer, and when it's frozen bust it up into little pieces, is how Puppy Pleasers taste.'

At the time I thought Charlie would either die of grit or slowly turn to sand from the feet up and I didn't know what we would do with him – stand him up in the backyard, maybe, and plant flowers around him.

I didn't know what the Herdmans would do with their dog, Howard, either. Whenever Charlie and I asked for a dog, my mother always said, 'What are you going to do with him?' and we never knew what to say. We thought the dog would do it all and we would just hang around and watch.

Mother said that's exactly what she *thought* we thought. 'When you find a dog that's smart enough to take care of itself and let itself in and out of the house and answer the phone, let me know,' she said.

Louella said we would have to watch Imogene, 'Or else she'll try to run off with Howard and take him home and name him some dog name, like Rover or Spot.'

Luckily, she never got the chance. Mrs. McCluskey got her wires crossed at the telephone company and shut down the whole system for half an hour. She never knew a thing like that could happen, she said, and it made her so nervous that she just quit her job, right on the spot. And after that Louella didn't have to bring Howard to school anymore.

This was a big relief to Louella and you could tell it made Miss Kemp happy too, but she gave a little speech anyway, about how we would miss Howard and how he would be a big part of our sixth-grade experience and how we would always remember him.

'Sounds like he died,' Imogene muttered. She was mad, I thought, because of wasting all her good deeds – getting Howard's blanket back and making kids leave him alone – and then not getting anything

139

for it, like a substitute dog, if that was what she wanted.

'There is one thing,' Miss Kemp went on. 'It seems Howard went off without his blanket. Has anyone seen Howard's blanket?'

No one had. Or else no one would *admit* they had, not with Imogene sitting there blowing this huge bubble of gum out and in and out and in, ready to park it on anyone who looked guilty. It's too bad you can't study bubble gum and get graded for it, because Imogene would get straight 'A's. Her bubbles were so big and so thin you could see her whole face through the bubble, like looking at somebody through their own skin.

'What if we can't find it?' I asked Louella.

'We better find it,' she said, 'or else Howard will go crazy because all he does is sob and cry and hold his breath and hiccup.'

He had also turned purple, she said, and he had almost passed out, so you had to figure that if somebody didn't turn up with Howard's blanket soon he would never make it to next week, let alone kindergarten.

We looked for the blanket off and on the rest of that day, although Alice said it would be better if we didn't find it. 'It's old and horrible and full of germs,' she said, and she told Louella, 'You should be glad it's lost. Howard will thank you someday.'

This is what your mother says when she makes you wear ugly shoes. She says, 'This will give your toes room to grow and you'll thank me someday.' Hearing

Alice say things like this makes you want to squirt her with canned cheese. Even Miss Kemp does, I think, because she said, 'Alice, I can assure you that by the time Howard gets to "someday", he won't even *remember* this blanket'.

Somebody muttered, 'Don't be too sure' – Imogene.

There was good news the next day – Howard have lived through the night without going crazy *or* purple – and even better news when Imogene showed up with his blanket. She said she found it at the bus stop underneath a bush.

Nobody believed this. The Herdmans stole everything that wasn't nailed down, just out of habit. Why not Howard's blanket? 'But so what?' Louella said, as long as Imogene brought it back.

The next day the art teacher, Miss Harrison, stopped Louella in the hall and gave her a bunch of stubby crayons for Howard. 'I just heard about your little brother's blanket,' she said. 'Louella, you aren't going to find it because I threw it away. The last time we had art I used it to wipe the pastels off the chalkboard and then I just threw it away. I'm really sorry, but I didn't know it was Howard's blanket. It looked like my car-washing rag.'

Louella shook her head. 'We found Howard's blanket.'

Miss Harrison shook *her* head. 'You're just saying that to make me feel better. No, as soon as I heard it was missing, I knew what I'd done and where it was – gone, in the trash.'

'She's wrong,' Louella said.

'Maybe you're wrong,' I said.

Louella thought for a minute. 'Well, Howard wouldn't be wrong and *he* thinks it's his blanket. You can't get it away from him.'

We did get it away from him but we had to wait till he was asleep. Then we had to unfasten his fingers and quickly give him this old worn-out bathrobe of Louella's.

'See?' said Louella. 'It's the same blanket.'

It certainly looked like the same blanket – old, faded, sort of dirty grey, with one corner that was especially old and faded and dirty grey. There was something else too – a capital *H*, scribbled and wobbly and almost faded out.

'It even has his initial on it,' I said. '*H*, for Howard.'

'Huh-uh,' Louella said. 'There's no initial on Howard's blanket.'

I started to show her the the *H*, and then I saw the *other* initial. It was an *I*.

I. H. There was only one *I. H.* in the whole Woodrow Wilson School – Imogene Herdman. 'Louella,' I said, 'Imogene didn't find this blanket underneath a bush or anywhere else. This was her *own* blanket.'

Louella refused to believe this and you couldn't blame her. It was hard enough just to imagine that Imogene ever *was* a baby, let alone a baby with her own blanket to drag around and hang on to.

'Besides,' Louella said, 'if it was hers, she wouldn't

give it away. The Herdmans never gave anything away in their whole life.'

'But what about the initials?' I said.

'They aren't really initials,' Louella said. 'I think they're just what's left of the bunny pattern.'

I guess Louella believed this, but I knew better. They were Imogene's initials, all right, and this was Imogene's blanket. Maybe somebody took it away from her when *she* was a baby, and maybe *she* yelled and held her breath and turned purple, so she would know exactly how Howard felt. She would be sympathetic.

I could hardly wait to write this down on the Compliments for Classmates page in my notebook, but it looked too weird: 'Imogene Herdman – sympathetic'.

Nobody would believe this and I would have to explain it and Imogene would probably wrap *my* head in chewing gum if I told everyone that she once had a blanket with a favourite chewed corner and everything.

CHAPTER EIGHT

Two or three times a year all the Herdmans would be absent at the same time and it was like a vacation. You knew you wouldn't get killed at recess, you wouldn't have to hand over your lunch, and you wouldn't have to hide your money if you had any.

We even had easy lessons when they were absent. Boomer Malone said the teachers did that on purpose to give us all time to heal and get our strength back, but my mother said it was probably the teachers who had to get their strength back.

Nobody knew why they were absent. Nobody cared. They didn't have to bring a note from home either like everyone else, to say what was the matter.

'Why bother?' the school nurse told my mother. 'They would write it themselves, no one could read it, and it would be a lie. Besides, if they ever did have something contagious, they wouldn't stay home. They'd come here and breathe on everybody.'

You never knew *when* they would be absent either, but nobody thought this made any difference till they were all absent on a fire-drill day and our school won the Fire Department Speed and Safety Award.

'I can't believe this improvement,' the fire chief

said. 'Last time it took you thirty-four minutes to vacate the building. What happened?'

'You know what happened,' Mr. Crabtree said. 'We lost half the kindergarten. Ollie Herdman led them out a basement door and took them all downtown.'

'I mean, what happened this time?'

'Nothing happened this time,' Mr. Crabtree said, 'because Ollie isn't here. Neither is Ralph or Imogene or Leroy or Claude or Gladys.'

'Where are they?'

'They're absent,' Mr. Crabtree said.

The chief sighed. 'I thought maybe they moved away. Oh, well . . .' He sighed again and said in that case he'd better get back to the firehouse and be ready for anything.

Everyone was pretty excited about the Speed and Safety Award, because we had never won anything before and probably never would again till the last Herdman was gone from Woodrow Wilson School.

So far, though, we could only be excited about the honour of it because we wouldn't get the actual award till Fire Prevention Day. There was a Fire Prevention Day every year, but all we ever got were Smokey the Bear stickers, so this was a big step up. There would be a special assembly with the fire chief and the mayor there, and the newspaper would send someone to take pictures and interview kids about fire prevention.

Of course fire prevention was the last thing the Herdmans knew anything about – except to be against it, I guess – so you had to hope the reporter wouldn't pick one of them to interview. You had to hope they wouldn't show up for this big event wearing beer advertisement T-shirts. You had to hope they wouldn't *show up.*

'Maybe they won't,' Charlie said. 'Maybe they don't even know we won the award.'

It's true that the Herdmans didn't know much if you count things like who invented the telephone, but they always knew what was going on around them, which in this case was plenty. There were signs and posters about fires and firemen everywhere; all the blackboards said 'Woodrow Wilson Elementary School, Speed and Safety Winner!' Kids were making bookmarks and placemats, and writing poems and stories about our big accomplishment. We didn't even have hot dogs and hamburgers at lunch – we had Fire Dogs and Smokey Burgers.

How could the Herdmans miss all this? They didn't.

Somebody in the second grade brought in this great big stuffed bear and they stood it up in the hall with a sign around its neck – 'Smokey says Con-gratulations to the Woodrow Wilson School!' – and the very next day there was the bear with its paws full of matches and cigarette lighters, firecrackers in its lap, and a half-smoked cigar sticking out of its mouth . . . Smokey, the Fire-Bug Bear.

'Oh, that is so disgusting!' Alice said. 'What if someone reports it to the fire department? We might not even get the award. As usual, they're going to mess everything up and ruin the whole assembly, hitting people and tripping people and folding little kids up in the seats!'

I guess Mr. Crabtree came in the back door that day and didn't know what had happened to the bear, because the first announcement was all about the outstanding fire-prevention display by the second grade. 'I want every student to stop by the second-grade room and see our very own Smokey the Bear,' he said, 'and let's be sure to thank those second graders for this . . .' Then there were some whispers and a *thwip* sound as somebody put a hand over the microphone, but you could still hear voices and a few words: ' . . . matches . . . horrible wet cigar . . . get rid of that bear . . .'

Then the secretary, Mrs. Parker, got on and shuffled some papers and cleared her throat and said that Mr. Crabtree had been called away suddenly and she would finish the announcements: picture money was due by Friday; a Fred Flintstone lunch box had been left on Bus 4; there would be a meeting of the Fire Safety Team in the lunchroom after school.

Right away Alice wrote this down on a piece of paper, as if she had so many important engagements that she *had* to write them all down.

Imogene poked me. 'What's the Fire Safety Team?'

'It's for the assembly,' I said. 'It's some kids who are going to demonstrate what to do in case of fire.'

Imogene shrugged. 'Throw water on it and get

out of the way.' Then she squinched up her eyes. 'What kids? Who's on this team?'

I was going to say 'I don't know' or 'Who cares' – something so loose that Imogene wouldn't want to waste her time – but as usual Alice had to blow her own horn.

'I am,' she said. 'There's ten of us plus two alternates in case somebody gets sick at the last minute.'

It's not unusual for people to get sick at the last minute if they're mixed up with Herdmans, so that got Imogene's attention, but it wasn't enough to hold her attention till Alice said, 'We're going to have T-shirts that say "Fire Safety Team, Woodrow Wilson School", so we'll all look alike in the picture.'

I didn't even bother to say 'Shut up, Alice' – it was too late. You could tell that Imogene was already seeing herself in the Fire Safety T-shirt *and* in the picture, and there was only one thing that you didn't know for sure – who, besides the two alternates, was going to get sick at the last minute.

Naturally Imogene wasn't the only Herdman who showed up in the lunchroom after school. They were all there, slouching around ready for action, draped over the tables, scraping gum from underneath the benches, chewing it – and this was *old* gum, shiny with germs and hard enough to tear your teeth out.

There was at least one kid from every grade on the Fire Safety Team and they all had one eye on the Herdmans, so Mr. Crabtree couldn't just *ignore* them, which is probably what he wanted to do.

'School's over, Ralph,' Mr. Crabtree said,

148

'Imogene, Ollie. Unless you people have some reason to be here, it's time to go home. We're just having a meeting.'

'We came to sign up,' Ralph said.

'Sign up for what? This is the Fire Safety Team.'

'Right,' Leroy said. 'That. We want to sign up for that.'

'It was on the announcements', Gladys put in, 'about the meeting after school.'

Mr. Crabtree opened his mouth and then he shut it again because there wasn't anything he could do about this. He had made it a major rule that anybody at the Woodrow Wilson School could sign up for anything they wanted to, no exceptions, and he had made another rule that everybody had to sign up for something whether they wanted to or not. So you had kids who signed up for two or three things, and you had kids who signed up for everything, and you had kids who wouldn't sign up at all till their teacher or their mother or Mr. Crabtree made them be something. What you didn't have was Herdmans signing up for anything.

Till now.

My mother said it was a good idea for the Herdmans to be on a Fire Safety Team. 'Who needs to know more about fire safety than those kids?' she said. Some people said at least this way you could keep an eye on them during the assembly. My father said it was like inviting a lot of bank robbers to demonstrate how to rob the bank.

Three kids quit the Fire Safety Team right away

before anything could happen to them, but their mothers said they ought to get the T-shirts anyway in view of the circumstances.

Mr. Crabtree knew what circumstances they were talking about – Herdmans – so he didn't even mention that. He just said he didn't have anything to do with the T-shirts. 'That's up to the PTA,' he said. 'The PTA is providing T-shirts for the Fire Safety Team in honour of this special occasion.'

The president of the PTA said they weren't providing T-shirts for kids who *quit* the Fire Safety Team. Mrs. Wendleken said they better not be providing T-shirts for the Herdmans, who had muscled their way *on to* the Fire Safety Team.

All anybody could talk about was T-shirts, but I agreed with Charlie, who said he wouldn't be on the Fire Safety Team if you paid him, not even for fifty T-shirts. 'I watched them practise,' he said, 'and when Mr. Crabtree yells "Drop and roll!" all the Herdmans drop *on* somebody, like in football.'

They dropped on Albert Pelfrey and nearly squashed him flat, which wasn't all bad because as I said Albert is this really fat kid, but Albert quit the Fire Safety Team anyway. 'I've got enough trouble just being fat,' he said. 'I don't want to be fat and dead both.'

At the last minute two kids got sick (or said they did) and right away both the alternates quit, which didn't surprise anybody.

'You don't want to quit,' Mr. Crabtree told them. 'This is a big opportunity.' He meant it was a big opportunity to take part in Fire Prevention Day and get a T-shirt and have their picture taken. But it was also a big opportunity to get pounded two feet into the ground by the Herdmans.

'I can only be an alternate,' Roberta Scott said. 'I can't actually be in it or anything.'

'Roberta, that's what an alternate *is*,' Mr. Crabtree said. 'It's your responsibility to be in it and everything. You too, Lonnie.'

Lonnie Hutchison was the other alternate, and he said he had to quit because of his asthma.

'Nice try, Lonnie,' Mr. Crabtree said, 'but you don't have asthma. I *know* who all has asthma. I know who has pinkeye and poison ivy and athlete's foot, also coughs and colds and nervous stomachs.'

Mr. Crabtree didn't mention any other diseases, and when Lonnie's mother called the school to say that Lonnie was sick with a rash, Mr. Crabtree didn't believe it.

'Too convenient,' he said. 'It's probably finger paint or Magic Marker, something like that. Two or three weeks ago I saw Leroy Herdman walking around with red spots all over *his* face, looking for trouble. I just told him, "Leroy, go wash your face," and the next time I saw him all the spots were gone.'

But it wasn't finger paint on Lonnie.

It was chicken pox, and before you could say 'Speed and Safety Award assembly' there wasn't anybody left to go to it.

Mr. Crabtree wanted to postpone Fire Prevention Day but the fire chief said he couldn't do that. 'It's

Fire Prevention Day all over town,' he said, 'all over the state. You can't just have your own Fire Prevention Day whenever you want to. Tell you what, though. If you'll get together a small group of whatever kids you've got left – your Fire Safety Team would be good – and bring them down to the firehouse, we'll have the award presentation right here. We'll make it a big event.'

It turned out to be a bigger event than anybody expected because the pizza-parlour ovens caught fire half an hour before the presentation. They put the fire out right away but Mr. Santoro made all his customers leave because of the smoke, and most of them just followed the fire engine back to the firehouse and stayed for the presentation. Some people thought the fire was *part* of the presentation, especially when Mr. Santoro showed up with all his leftover pizza and handed it out free.

Everybody said this was a great way to advertise fire prevention, and they congratulated the mayor and the fire chief for thinking it up, and the fire chief congratulated Mr. Santoro for donating the pizza.

The newspaper report got it all wrong too. 'MOCK FIRE STAGED TO HIGHLIGHT FIRE PREVENTION DAY', he wrote. 'RESTAURANT OWNER CONTRIBUTES PIZZA FOR LARGE CROWD ATTENDING AWARD CEREMONY. SCHOOL STUDENTS HONOURED FOR SAFETY TECHNIQUES'.

The 'honoured students' were what was left of the Fire Safety Team – Ralph, Imogene, Leroy, Claude, Ollie, and Gladys – and there was a picture of them standing in front of the fire truck, looking like a police lineup. You could imagine an officer saying, 'Now, which one did it?' and the victim saying, 'I can't be sure. They all look alike.'

They did look alike, except for being different sizes . . . plus, of course, they had on the famous matching T-shirts.

'If I didn't know better,' Mother said, 'I would think this was the Herdmans being honoured instead of the school.'

This turned out to be the general opinion, and so many people called the newspaper to complain that they printed another story – 'WOODROW WILSON SCHOOL, DESPITE CHICKEN POX EPIDEMIC, WINS SPEED AND SAFETY AWARD', which my father said was better than nothing, but not much. 'What does chicken pox have to do with it?' he wanted to know, but my mother said he was just tired of watching Charlie and me scratch.

Mrs. Wendleken made Alice sit in a bathtub full of baking-soda water so she wouldn't scratch, and made her wear these white cotton gloves so she wouldn't scratch, and when Alice came back to school, besides having puckery seersucker skin, she was still wearing the gloves.

'I don't think that's necessary, Alice,' Miss Kemp said.

'I have to wear them while I'm thinking,' Alice told her, 'so I won't forget and scratch. If you scratch chicken pox, they get infected and leave scars.'

'Not on Leroy,' Imogene said. 'Not on Ollie. Not on . . .'

'Wait a minute,' Miss Kemp said. 'Leroy? Ollie? I wasn't aware that any of your family was absent during our epidemic.'

'Oh, we weren't absent,' Imogene said.

Miss Kemp frowned. 'But you had chicken pox?' she asked.

'You mean, did I have chicken pox?' Imogene said.

This was like talking long distance to my grandmother without her hearing aid, and – just like my grandmother – Miss Kemp didn't try to pin it down.

'If you have chicken pox, you can't come back without a note from the doctor,' she said, and Imogene said, 'Oh. Okay,' and got up and left.

So no one ever knew for sure whether they did actually have chicken pox, or how many of them had chicken pox, and no one ever knew for sure whether they came to school and breathed on everybody and ruined our big award assembly, or whether they were all sick and stayed home on the fire-drill day so we won the award in the first place.

CHAPTER NINE

The last day of school is pretty loose and they probably wouldn't even bother to have one except that that's when you clean out your desk. If you didn't have to clean out your desk, Mr. Crabtree could just get on the PA system any old day in June and say, 'All right, this is it, last day of school. Go on home. Have a great summer. See you in September.'

But then everyone would go off and leave their smelly old socks and mouldy mittens and melted Halloween candy and leftover sandwiches. Once a kindergarten gerbil got loose and climbed in Boomer Malone's desk and died there.

Nobody knew what to do with the gerbil because, like all the kindergarten animals, it had a name and a personality and we knew all about it from the notice on the bulletin board – 'Our friendly gerbil is missing. His name is Bob. If you see Bob, please return him to the kindergarten room.'

So this wasn't just any old dead gerbil – this was friendly Bob. It didn't seem right to drop him in the trash, so Boomer took him back to the kindergarten room. We all thought the kindergarten would stop whatever it was doing, hunt up a cigar box, write a poem for Bob, and have a funeral, but according to Boomer they couldn't care less.

'Not even the teacher,' he reported. 'She took one look and said, "Oh, that's not Bob," and dropped him in her trash basket.'

If there was a moral to this, I guess it was: Don't show up with dead animals on the last day of school.

You couldn't show up with live ones either anymore. We used to have a pet parade every year on the last day of school, till the year Claude Herdman entered their cat.

The Herdmans' cat was missing one eye and part of an ear and most of its tail and all of whatever good nature it ever had, so you wouldn't expect it to win any prizes in a pet parade. If it was your cat, you would probably try to clean it up a little, but you probably wouldn't whitewash it and then spray it with super-super-hold hairspray, which is what the Herdmans did.

According to Claude, they thought it would win the Most Unusual Pet prize, but it was too mad from being whitewashed and hairsprayed to do anything but attack. So the pet parade turned into a stampede of dogs and cats and turtles and hamsters and guinea pigs. Some kids held on to their animals but most didn't, so there were cats up in the trees and on top of telephone poles, and dogs running off down the street, barking . . . and the Herdmans' cat in the middle of it all, tearing around the playground, hissing and spitting and shedding flakes of white-wash. It took all day to get the cats down and the dogs back, and there were two hamsters that never did turn up.

So that was the end of the pet parade, and it left a big empty spot in the day's activities, which the teachers had to fill up somehow. We had spelling bees and math marathons, or we stood up and said what we were going to do that summer, or what we would do if we were king of the world.

One year everybody brought their collections. There were baseball cards and Cracker Jack prizes and bubble-gum wrappers . . . and belly-button lint.

The belly-button lint came from Imogene Herdman, but she said she wouldn't recommend it as a hobby. 'I don't even collect it anymore,' she said. 'This is left over from when I *used* to collect it.' I guess that was the last straw – old belly-button lint – because we never did that again.

This year there was no big surprise about what we would do on the last day. It was up on the blackboard – Compliments for Classmates – and we had each drawn a name from a hat and had to think of more compliments for that one person.

'We've been thinking about this all year,' Miss Kemp said. She probably knew that some kids had but most kids hadn't – but now everybody would think about it in a hurry. 'And on the last day of school,' she went on, 'we're going to find out what we've learned about ourselves and each other.'

I had finally thought of a word for Albert. Once you get past thinking *fat* you can see that Albert's special quality is optimism, because Albert actually believes he will be thin someday, and says so. Another word could be *determination*, or even *courage*. There were lots of good words for Albert, so I really hoped I would draw his name.

I didn't. The name I drew was Imogene Herdman, and I had used up the one and only compliment I finally thought of for Imogene – *patriotic*.

'Patriotic?' my mother said. 'What makes you think Imogene is especially patriotic?'

'When we do the Pledge of Allegiance,' I said, 'she always stands up.'

'Everybody stands up,' Charlie said. 'If everybody sat down and *only* Imogene stood up, that would be patriotic.'

'That would be brave,' I said.

'Well, she would do that,' Charlie said. 'I mean, she would do whatever everybody else didn't do.'

Would that make Imogene brave? I didn't really think so, but I had to have some more compliments, so I wrote it down – *patriotic, brave.*

Two days later I still had just *patriotic* and *brave* while other people had big long lists. I saw the bottom of Joanne Turner's list, sticking out of her notebook: 'Cheerful, good sport, graceful, fair to everybody'. I wondered who *that* was.

Maxine Cooper asked me how to spell *cooperative* and *enthusiastic*, so obviously she had a terrific list. Boomer must have drawn a boy's name, because all his compliments came right out of the Boy Scout Rules – *thrifty, clean, loyal.*

I kept my eye on Imogene as much as possible so if

she did something good I wouldn't miss it, but it was so hard to tell, with her, what was good.

I thought it was good that she got Boyd Liggett's head out of the bike rack, but Mrs. Liggett didn't think so.

Mrs. Liggett said it was all the Herdmans' fault in the first place. 'Ollie Herdman told Boyd to do it,' she said, 'and then that Gladys got him so scared and nervous that he couldn't get out, and then along came Imogene . . .'

I could understand how Boyd got his head *into* the bike rack – he's only in the first grade, plus he has a skinny head – but at first I didn't know why he couldn't get it *out*.

Then I saw why. It was his ears. Boyd's ears stuck right straight out from his head like handles, so his head and his ears were on one side of the bike rack and the rest of him was on the other side, and kids were hollering at him and telling him what to do. 'Turn your head upside down!' somebody said, and somebody else told him to squint his eyes and squeeze his face together.

Boyd's sister Jolene tried to fold his ears and push them through but that didn't work, even one at a time. Then she wanted half of us to get in front of him and push and the other half to get in back and pull. 'He got his head through there,' she said. 'There must be some way to get it back out.'

I didn't think pushing and pulling was the way but Boyd looked ready to try anything.

Then Gladys Herdman really cheered him up.

'Going to have to cut off your ears, Boyd,' she said. 'But maybe just one ear. Do you have a favourite one? That you like to hear out of?'

You could tell that he believed her. If you're in the first grade with your head stuck through the bike rack, this is the very thing you think will happen.

Several teachers heard Boyd yelling, 'Don't cut my ears off!' and they went to tell Mr. Crabtree. Mr. Crabtree called the fire department, and while he was doing that the kindergarten teacher stuck her head out the window and called to Boyd, 'Don't you worry, they're coming to cut you loose.'

But she didn't say who, or how, and Gladys told him they would probably leave a little bit of ear in case he ever had to wear glasses, so Boyd was a total wreck when Imogene came along.

She wanted to know how he got in there – in case she ever wanted to shove somebody else in the bike rack, probably – but Boyd was too hysterical to tell her, and nobody else knew for sure, so I guess she decided to get him loose first and find out later.

Imogene Scotch-taped his ears down and buttered his whole head with soft margarine from the lunch-room, and then she just pushed on his head – first one side and then the other – and it slid through.

Of course Boyd was a mess, with butter all over his eyes and ears and up his nose, so Jolene had to take him home. She made him walk way away from her and she told him, 'As soon as you see Mother, you yell, "I'm all right. I'm all right." ' She looked at him again. 'You better tell her who you are, too.'

Even so, Mrs. Liggett took one look and screamed
and would have fainted, Jolene said, except she heard
Boyd telling her that he was all right.

'What do you think of that?' Mother asked my
father that night. 'She buttered his head!'

'I think it was resourceful,' my father said. 'Messy,
but resourceful.'

'That's like a compliment, isn't it?' I asked my
father. 'It's good to be resourceful?'

'Certainly,' he said. So I wrote that down, along
with *patriotic* and *brave*.

I thought we would just hand in our compliment
papers on the last day of school, but Alice thought
Miss Kemp would read three or four out loud –
'Some of the best ones,' Alice said, meaning, of
course, her own – and Boomer thought she would
read the different compliments and we would have to
guess the person. So when Miss Kemp said, 'Now
we're going to share these papers,' it was no big
surprise.

But then she said, 'I think we'll start with Boomer.
LaVerne Morgan drew your name, Boomer. I want
you to sit down in front of LaVerne and listen to
what she says about you.'

La Verne squealed and Boomer turned two or
three different shades of red and all over the room
kids began to check their papers in case they would
have to read out loud some big lie or, worse, some
really personal compliment.

LaVerne said that Boomer was smart and good at
sports – but not stuck up about it – and friendly, and

two or three other normal things. 'And I liked when you took the gerbil back to the kindergarten that time,' she said, 'in case they wanted to bury it. That was nice.'

It *was* nice, I thought, and not everybody would have done it, either. To begin with, not everybody would have *picked up* the gerbil by what was left of its tail, let alone carry it all the way down the hall and down the stairs to the kindergarten room.

'Good, Boomer,' I said when he came back to his seat – glad to get there, I guess, because he was all sweaty with embarrassment from being told nice things about himself face to face and in front of everybody.

Next came Eloise Albright and then Louella and then Junior Jacobs and then Miss Kemp said, 'Let's hear about you, Beth. Joanne Turner drew your name.'

I remembered Joanne Turner's paper – 'Cheerful, good sport, graceful, fair to everybody'. I had wondered who that was.

It was me.

'I know we weren't supposed to say things about how you look,' Joanne said, 'but I put down graceful anyway because I always notice how you stand up very straight and walk like some kind of dancer. I don't know if you can keep it up, but if you can I think people will always admire the way you stand and walk.'

It was really hard, walking back to my seat now that I was famous for it – but I knew if I did it now, with everybody watching, I *could* probably keep it up for the rest of my life and, if Joanne was right, be admired forever. This made me feel strange and loose and light, like when you press your hands hard against the sides of a door, and when you walk away your hands float up in the air all by themselves.

I was still feeling that way three people later when Miss Kemp said it was Imogene's turn.

'To do what?' Imogene said.

'To hear what Beth has to say about you. She drew your name.'

Imogene gave me this dark, suspicious look. 'No, I don't want to.'

'You're going to hear *good* things, you know, Imogene,' Miss Kemp said, but you could tell Miss Kemp wasn't too sure about that, and Imogene probably never *heard* any good things about herself, so she wasn't too sure, either.

'That's okay,' I said. 'I mean, if Imogene doesn't want to, I don't care.'

This didn't work. I guess Miss Kemp was curious like everybody else. 'Imogene Herdman!' Louella had just whispered. 'That's whose name you drew? How could you think of compliments for Imogene Herdman?'

'Well, you had to think of *one*,' I said. 'We had to think of one compliment for everybody.'

Louella rolled her eyes. 'I said she was healthy. I didn't know anything else to say.'

Louella wasn't the only one who wanted to hear my Imogene words. The whole room got very quiet and I was glad, now, that at the last minute I had looked up *resourceful* in the dictionary.

'I put down that you're patriotic,' I told Imogene, 'and brave and resourceful . . . and cunning and shrewd and creative, and enterprising and sharp and inventive . . .'

'Wait!' she yelled. 'Wait a minute! Start over!'

'Oh, honestly!' Alice put in. 'You just copied that out of the dictionary! They're all the same thing!'

'And,' I went on, ignoring Alice, 'I think it was good that you got Boyd's head out of the bike rack.'

'Oh, honestly!' Alice said again, but Miss Kemp shut her up.

Of course she didn't say, 'Shut up, Alice' – she just said that no one could really comment on what anybody else said because it was very personal and individual. 'That's how Beth sees Imogene,' she said.

Actually, it wasn't. Alice was right about the words. I did copy them out of the dictionary so I wouldn't be the only person with three dumb compliments, and I didn't exactly connect them with Imogene, except *sharp* because of her knees and elbows which she used like weapons to leave you black and blue.

But now, suddenly, they all turned out to fit. Imogene *was* cunning and shrewd. She *was* inventive. Nobody else thought of buttering Boyd's head or washing their cat at the Laundromat. She was creative, if you count drawing pictures on Howard . . . and enterprising, if you count charging money to look at him. She was also powerful enough to keep everybody away from the teachers' room forever, and human enough to give Howard her blanket.

Imogene *was* all the things I said she was, and more, and they were good things to be – depending on who it was doing the inventing or the creating or the enterprising. If Imogene could keep it up, I thought, till she got to be civilized, if that ever happened, she could be almost anything she wanted to be in life.

She could be Imogene Herdman, President Imogene or, of course, Imogene Herdman, Jailbird. It would be up to her.

At the end of the day Miss Kemp said, 'Which was harder – to give compliments or to receive them?' and everyone agreed that it was really uncomfortable to have somebody tell you, in public, about the best hidden parts of you. Alice, however, made this long, big-word speech about how it was harder for her to *give* compliments because she wanted to be very accurate and truthful, 'and not make things up,' she said, looking at me.

'I didn't make things up,' I told her later, except, maybe, brave. I don't know whether Imogene is brave.'

'You made her sound like some wonderful person,' Alice said, 'and if that's not making things up, what is?'

When the bell rang everybody whooped out to get started on summer, but Imogene grabbed me in the hall, shoved a Magic Marker in my face, and told me to write the words on her arm.

'On your arm?' I said.

'That's where I keep notes,' she said, and I could believe it because I could still see the remains of several messages – something pizza . . . big rat . . . get Gladys . . .

Get Gladys something? I wondered. No, probably just get Gladys.

There was only room for one word on her skinny arm, so Imogene picked *resourceful*. 'It's the best one,' she said. 'I looked it up and I like it. It's way better than graceful, no offence.' She turned her arm around, admiring the word. 'I like it a lot. I'm gonna get it tattooed.'

I didn't ask who by – Gladys, probably.

Charlie was waiting for me on the corner, looking gloomy. He always looks gloomy on the last day of school, and it's always for the same reason.

'It happened again,' he said. 'Leroy Herdman didn't get kept back.'

'Leroy Herdman will never be kept back,' I told him. 'None of them will.'

'He's going to be in my room forever!' he groaned. 'What am I going to do?'

'Charlie,' I said, 'you're going to have to learn to be . . . resourceful.'

'How?' he said. 'What is it?'

'Ask Imogene,' I said. 'I think it's going to be her best thing.'

WASIM IN THE DEEP END

Chris Ashley

CHAPTER ONE

Wasim had to be first.

'Oy, Wasim!'

'Wasim! Miss, he's knocked my graph off the wall.'

Wasim, first at the door and staring like a guardsman at 110 cm on the height chart, spun round as fast as his bulging United rucksack would let him.

'Tell him, Miss.'

Wasim had to be first whenever there was a line, but today was special. Today was swimming day – the last swimming day.

Today Wasim really had to be first and somebody, Ben Perry it sounded like, was trying to ruin it by getting him done. Wasim would get sent to the back and time would be wasted.

The last swimming day, free time for most groups and for Wasim's group, the splash group, the chance to do their One Star. From the steps at the deep end to the steps at the shallow end, twenty-five metres. And then on Friday there'd be Mr. Abbott in the sharing assembly, doing his television voice while he gave out the certificate. *'Wasim Ahmed,'* he'd say *'You're a star.'*

A One Star, that was what it was, a big red star on your certificate.

Twenty-five metres – gulping, spluttering, no armbands – a red star on a piece of card. One Star.

There was a sharp dig in Wasim's back. Ben was trying once again,

'*Miss?*'

'*Oh, just be sensible for one minute,*' Mrs. Scott snapped. Wasim couldn't believe his luck and he turned back to the height chart. Miss was still busy with the dinner money.

'*But, Miss, he's pushed in and knocked –*'

'*Ben, I am busy!*'

Wasim stared even harder at the height chart and waited until his senses told him that Mrs. Scott had turned back to the pile of Monday money on her desk. Then he allowed himself the flare of his nostrils and the '*Sss . . . sss . . . sss,*' that would send Ben barmy.

'*Miss! He's laughing, Miss. Just because –*'

Mrs. Scott finally bashed the Tuppaware container they all called the money tin onto the table.

'*OK, Ben,*' she was saying in a whisper that sounded louder than one of Mr. Abbott's shouts. '*Since you have such a problem with Wasim you had better go and be Neil's partner. Go on.*'

Wasim gave a secret flare of his nostrils. Neil was nowhere near the front. A scowling Ben began pushing his way back.

'*And er, Eric, you go up with Wasim.*'

Mrs. Scott paused and then said it more carefully. *'Eric, you go with Wasim.'*

But Wasim was going to sort it out. Eric Ho was new. He was new to the school and new to the country. He didn't speak much English yet and Wasim knew what it was like when you had different words for things at home.

He knew what it was like when the only school word you knew was Miss. What you needed was someone like him, Wasim, to help you out. He barged back down the line, accidentally brushing two graphs onto the floor with his rucksack, and pulled Eric up to the front.

'Oy, Wasim!'

'Ahmed!'

But they were only breathing it now because Miss was looking down at the money and they were late already.

Wasim stood at attention again and waited. He nudged at Eric until the new boy stood at attention too. Then he stared again at 110 cm and thought about his One Star. Twenty-five metres and no armbands!

CHAPTER TWO

Finally, Junior S got away.

Mrs. Scott had seen the graphs and looked at Wasim, her eyes never leaving his while she bent down, picked them up and put them silently onto the bookshelf next to the display.

'*Don't worry, I'll pick them up*,' she said. Which meant that somebody else should have.

'*Miss, it wasn't –* '

But Mrs. Scott wasn't saying any more and that told Wasim to stop. He'd have to show that he was a particularly good leader on the walk, though. Especially when it came to not following Miss into the road. Nicola Harris had forgotten last week and not waited for the signal to follow.

'*Stop there*! *How many times* . . .?'

Mrs. Scott had shouted. She didn't shout often, but she did when it came to roads. Even at Nicola Harris.

Wasim led them in silence down past the assembly and allowed himself a glance through the hall door at the piano where the certificates would be piled.

Then he walked importantly on. He smiled at Eric. Things were going well.

He did his special walk under the subway. It was

fast but you didn't run, and at each kerb he put a hand out to stop Eric and sensibly waited for Mrs. Scott, who seemed a bit out of breath.

'*Eric's not your real name, is it?*' Samantha Waterworth shouted from behind. '*Doesn't sound right with Ho, and when you're Chinese or Japanese . . .*'

'*Hong Kong he comes from, don't you, Eric?*' Gemma came right up beside them. '*Miss said so.*'

Wasim pushed her back into her place. It was his job to talk to Eric. '*Shut up, Waterworth,*' he said.

'*You shut up, Wasim. Miss!*'

But Mrs. Scott was still puffing to keep up with Wasim's special walk and she pretended not to hear. Wasim quickly got chatting before she changed her mind.

'*Are you in our group – splash group?*'

Eric just smiled, friendly. He didn't say a lot.

Wasim tried it in his own home words, Urdu, whispering in case Gemma took the mickey out of it. But Eric just smiled again.

'*D'you have armbands? You'll be with us.*'

Eric looked puzzled, so Wasim mimed armbands and followed Mrs. Scott into the road.

'*Wasim Ahmed!*'

Wasim jumped and scuttled back to Eric on the pavement, saying, '*So?*' before Gemma had a chance to say anything. He pushed his glasses up and finally allowed himself to meet Mrs. Scott's glare.

'*Do not step off the pavement until I signal. Is that clear?*'

'*Miss!*'

Of course it was clear, he was the best in the class at knowing that. '*So?*' he hissed at no one in particular.

Wasim felt somebody laughing behind him, but Mrs. Scott was still looking at him and they were crossing the road now which meant he couldn't do anything anyway. So for the last few streets Wasim just thought about the steps, the steps up at the deep end. The rough plastic on the soles of his feet, the slow cool that would spread up his legs as he went down and then make his chest stop thumping as it spread over his tummy.

Then there would be the terrible moment when John the swimming teacher made him let go. He'd feel nothingness under his feet and then the cool would become cold and move up to his throat and his mouth would start gasping and his legs would start wriggling and . . . and that was all he knew. Last time that he had been all there was to it. Wasim had stopped going down and suddenly felt like he was flying. Well he was in a way, he was floating. He'd had armbands on but straight away Andrew Foster had jumped in behind him and told him to shove up. So he'd wriggled and gulped and spluttered up to the shallow end. 'Miss!' he'd shouted when he got there. And Mrs. Scott had put her hands above her head and clapped. That was last time!

A warm smell of feet hit Wasim and he put a hand out to stop Eric. That was the swimming smell.

One more corner. Now Wasim's stomach started turning again. What if he didn't float? What if his

174

legs didn't start kicking and he didn't start reaching and pulling like John and Dad kept telling him? What if he didn't do it and had to grab the pole before he got to the shallow steps?

'*Oy, Wasim, move it. What you stopped for?*' and there was a push as the line came to a spluttering halt and Eric was bundled into him. What if he didn't do it?

'*Ahmed!*' came another shout.

Wasim began to walk again and found that his mouth was too dry even to tell Gemma to shut up. He'd do it . . . wouldn't he? Twenty-five metres. No armbands.

CHAPTER THREE

The big glass doors opened and the smell of feet, Dettol and chloreysomething filled Wasim's head and got mixed up with shouts half echoed and then lost in distant splashes. Blue glittered and danced on the ceiling, teasing the children about what they would see behind the big window as soon as Mrs. Scott had finished signing them in. Wasim had to put his hands in his pockets to stop himself from pushing her, but finally they were in.

'*First look!*' Wasim had spun round to say it and there it was, the pool – blue and beautiful and long, very long. One Star long.

'*Second!*' said Samantha.

'*First worst!*' shouted Gemma. But it wasn't being nasty, they were all too happy.

Wasim wanted to be first into the Boys, to get the best peg next to the warm door, but Eric had walked on and was following Gemma and Samantha. Some of the boys, crushing through their door, started laughing.

'*Eric's going into the Girls!*' they cried and tried those whistles where you put your fingers into your mouth. Wasim would miss the warm peg. He thought for a second but then he elbowed his way out. Eric needed him, he remembered, and being first wouldn't matter today, not One Star day. He rushed up the corridor.

'*Eric, Eric!*' The shouts bouncing off the tiles and the hot chocolate machine.

'*Do not shout in my pool!*'

Everyone froze. It was Carol, the other swimming teacher, the younger one, coming out of her room. The girls all said they liked her – but that was just because she looked like Vixen on *Gladiators*. She just screamed at everyone all the time and Wasim was really glad that she didn't take the splash group.

She glared down at Wasim. '*Do you behave like that all the time? I'd hate to live in your house.*'

Carol made it sound as if living in Wasim's house would be the worst thing in the world and he wasn't sure that it was just because of his shouting.

'*Problem?*' Mrs. Scott was there and Wasim felt safe again, just like he always did in school.

'*Miss, M . . .*' Wasim couldn't explain quickly enough.

'*Miss, Eric was going into the Girls,*' Nicola said.

'*Oh, he's never been to the baths before. Come on, Eric.*'

Carol glared at Wasim and he could tell she was cross that Miss hadn't joined in telling him off. She banged through the swing door and the splashes and shouts that came through from the pool hit Wasim like a great wave.

'*Miss, what group is Eric in?*' Gemma asked, still giggling.

'*Non-swimmers*,' replied Mrs. Scott. '*We've sorted this all out with Mum, haven't we, Eric?*'

Eric smiled.

'*Eric's in the non-swimmers.*'

'*But what if he can swim his Three Star or the Bronze or something, Miss?*'

'*It doesn't matter if you can swim to the moon. Until I see you swim, you're a non-swimmer and you stay in the shallow end.*'

The girls giggled going through their red door and Mrs. Scott turned to Wasim. 'Stay with him, Wasim. Splash group, is that clear?'

'Miss.'

Wasim felt tall and excited again now. He put an arm around Eric to lead him into the Boys and gave him a thumbs up. Eric gave one back. That seemed to work.

Wasim wouldn't have got the best hook anyway. A group from the High School were in and all of the boys from Wasim's class were getting changed in silence, just listening to the big ones and keeping out of their way. The older ones had hold of one kid's trunks and were throwing them around.

Wasim nodded to a hook and he and Eric got changed quickly, ducking whenever the wet trunks were thrown near them.

'*Quick as you can, lads.*' John came in from the pool. The High School kids pretended to get dressed sensibly and the boy who owned the trunks went and picked them up as if it were his fault they were on the floor. The swimming teacher must have known something was going on because he stayed, arms folded, foot tapping. The relieved Junior S boys got changed at double speed and skidded under his towering figure. Then it was up the steps, through the footbath and the freezing showers, and onto the poolside.

Wasim was third ready. Not bad considering. But he waited for Eric. He showed his new friend how to dodge the shower spray and then he too was on the poolside. He blanked out the noises and splashes, and shivered. It was not just that a few drops of the shower had hit him, it was also because he was looking at the two sets of steps. He'd seen them a hundred times before but never like today. Never when they meant so much. Never when he would have to grab that round, glittering steel, watch his face turn into funny shapes on its shiny surface and then let himself drop into the blue. Never when getting between the ones up near the Girls and the ones at the shallow end meant everything.

'*Wasim Ahmed . . . You're a star.*'

That would be Friday.

Wasim hugged himself.

He'd do it, he'd do it. And then the whistle blew.

'*Right, splash group, yes? You've got me today. John's with the High School.*'

Oh no, Wasim thought. Not Carol. Not Carol for his One Star.

CHAPTER FOUR

'*Do not run!*'

There were nine of them left once the Two Star, Three Star and Bronze groups had walked off with their floats for free time. The nine were non-swimmers . . . until today. By the end of today, some of them – most of them – would be One Stars, swimmers.

Eric had begun to follow the others but Mrs. Scott, in her pumps, had been walking round ready to look after her group up at the deep end. 'No, Eric. You stay here in the shallow end until we can see what you can do.' She pointed to where Wasim was standing and Eric, who did everything that he under-stood first time, came and stood with Wasim.

There was a huge cheer from the deep end as the other groups dived, jumped and bombed into the water. The splash group grinned at each other. They'd be in any second now. Wasim could almost taste the water as he imagined his special jump and spit out. Then, once they were used to the water, they'd go up for the twenty-five metre swim.

Wasim gave Eric another thumbs up and waited. Come on. Come on. Carol was talking and they hadn't been told to get in yet. She was with one of the lifeguards in his bright yellow polo shirt and shorter than short shorts. He was leaning against the wall and she was laughing. Come on . . . come on.

At last the lifeguard went back to his special seat at the 1.5 metre mark. The splash group looked at each other again and some hopeful smiles broke out.

But then the yellow shirt turned and said something about a rota which Carol didn't seem to like. She put her hands on her hips and started talking again. Nine pairs of eyes pleaded with each other and Andrew looked up at the clock and flashed his hands twice. '*Twenty minutes,*' he mouthed.

Then Gemma spoke up. Good old Gemma, thought Wasim. She wasn't so bad. '*Miss? When are we going in?*'

Carol turned and looked as if someone had stabbed her with a spear or something. '*When . . . I . . . am . . . good . . . and . . . ready.*'

But Gemma would probably look like Vixen herself one day and Carol usually liked her. Carol raised her eyes to the heavens and then looked at the splash group as if she was doing them a big favour.

'*It's free time, isn't it? Go and choose yourselves a float each,*' she said and turned back to yellow shirt.

Donna and Jamila nudged each other and skipped off. Nobody else moved. The One Star. Who was going to say something about the One Star? Gemma wasn't, she was already shaking her head. Wasim took a deep breath . . . but then he let it out. Why should it be him? But the others had seen it and knew there

181

was a chance of him doing it. Andrew was nudging him and Gemma had her hands on her hips and her eyebrows raised.

Wasim gulped in another breath. '*Miss . . . Miss . . . Miss . . .*' It still happened when he was excited. '*Miss*' was all that would come out.

'You are going to get on my nerves, young man. Choose your floats. Are you disobeying me?'

'*Miss . . . M . . .*'

Carol turned purple, but Wasim was going to get it out. '*Miss . . . we've got to do our One Star, Miss.*'

There was silence. Even the shrieks from the kids in the water seemed to stop. The lifeguard gave Carol a look and walked off to his chair. But he didn't sit in it. He looked back to see what Carol would do.

'*And who says?*'

That was it. They all knew it then. Carol wasn't going to let them do it!

'*John said, Miss.*' It was Gemma and they all looked at her. Wasim decided he was going to give her his prawn cocktail crisps after. '*John said last week, Miss.*'

Nothing happened. Gemma knew what she was doing. John was in charge, he ran the pool. They all knew he was above Carol. Nothing happened. Donna and Jamila climbed in and started jumping up and down keeping their heads out of the water. The rest of them waited. Eric looked puzzled.

'*Do not move.*'

They weren't going to. Carol gave them a last glare and, arms folded to show she was taking her time, she walked in slow motion to where John was crouching next to the group of High School children. The splash group watched as John looked up. No one breathed. Carol's arm flapped in their direction and, shivering again, Wasim tried to swallow.

John was looking at them and . . .

John was nodding. Yes, yes, yes!

John was nodding.

Carol, her arms still folded, began a long, slow walk back while they all looked at the floor in case she saw them being pleased. Wasim, though, looked up through his eyebrows and managed to meet Andrew's eyes. He flared his nostrils wide and he could see Andrew killing himself not to laugh. Wasim hoped he wouldn't as that really would ruin it.

Carol got back to them and snatched a pole from the wall. They were going. 'Not a sound,' was all she said and she led the way up towards the steps while Wasim looked at every tile on the bottom and tried to imagine every droplet of water as he began the twenty-five metre walk that in a few seconds he would be trying to swim.

He'd let somebody else be first, he decided, just for once. Somebody overtook. Let them, thought Wasim. It was Eric, his straight cropped hair bouncing as he walked.

No, Eric wouldn't be doing his One Star, would he? He hadn't even done his width for Miss yet. No, no, he should be down there with Donna and Jamila.

Wasim tapped Eric's back. Eric turned and smiled.

Wasim thrust his thumb back in the direction of the shallow end. Eric kept walking. '*Back!*' said Wasim, but it was too quiet. '*Back!*' he hissed. But this time it was too loud. He knew before it had finished coming out that it was too loud and yes, Carol had stopped.

'*Right. I don't even need to ask who that was, do I? I said silence and I am already more than fed up with you.*'

'*M . . . Miss . . .*'

But she had turned, dangerously slowly, and was almost at the steps now. Wasim had to tell Eric without talking. Wasim tapped him. Eric ignored it. He knew what getting in trouble meant and Carol's mood was Carol's mood in every language in the world. So Wasim did it. He grabbed Eric's shoulders, turned him round and tried to push him back to the shallow end. Eric, looking hurt, broke free and turned back. Wasim tried again. He reached out, got Eric's shoulders and . . . it was then that Carol turned round.

All the smells, all the sounds, all the colours and Eric's hurt, puzzled face, they all crowded in on Wasim and got jumbled up. Only one thing was clear. It was one of Carol's words in between all the stuff she was shouting about Wasim fighting in the line. It echoed through his head and it made him feel sick. It was, '*Out!*' She'd said, '*Out!*' and she was pointing at the changing room. '*Out!*' The pool was silent now. '*Out. You'll have to do it next week.*'

Wasim tried to breathe. There wasn't a next week, it was the holidays. This was it until his class's turn next year.

Wasim found that he had carried on walking. He was the only person moving in the whole pool. He was right up with her now. He'd explain. '*Miss, M . . .*' He needed time for the right words. '*Miss.*'

But Carol wasn't going to give him any time. '*Out! Out!*'

So that was it. Wasim turned, a huge sob was coming up and he had to get out before it exploded out of his mouth and down his nose. He turned and walked with his elbows pumping, glaring at the ground, then at them all, at Eric and at Gemma.

'*So?*' he managed to spit at Donna looking up at him from the shallow end. And then he'd finished his walk and he was past the steps.

Twenty-five metres. No armbands and no One Star.

CHAPTER FIVE

Wasim did what he always did first and put on his glasses. But he was crying now, sitting on the bench under his hook really sobbing and so his glasses just steamed up . . . useless. A huge rolling tickle went through him and he wanted to hit something or throw something or scream out loud. Then he thought of tonight, going in through his front door and not being able to tell them that he'd done it, passed.

He wanted home now, Mum and Dad, Shamaila his little sister and Atif his brother. He thought about his house and all the love that was in it. His house and how Carol had said she'd hate to live there. Well, he'd hate to have her there . . . How dare she say that. He'd never let her in his house and he knew why she'd really hate to live there. Well, he couldn't be sure but . . .

Wasim took his glasses off and wiped them while he thought of his dad taking time off to practise swimming on the last two Saturdays. He was cold. He pulled his towel from his rucksack and a piece of paper fell out. Wasim wiped his glasses again and picked it out of the puddle. His glasses were still no good so he squinted and read it without them.

'*Good luck.*'

Wasim heaved again in a great gulp.

'*What's that say, then? That's not English.*'

Wasim jumped, startled.

'*What's it say?*' The kid was coming over. He was from the High School, the small one whose trunks the others had thrown around.

'*Nothing.*' Wasim stuffed the note back into his bag.

'*Please yourself. What's up with you, then?*'

Wasim pulled his bag down and began searching for his shirt. He could remember stuffing it down there somewhere.

'*You the one that got chucked out?*'

'*So?*' Wasim searched harder to stop the tears coming again.

'*They nicked my trunks so I can't go in, can I. We were doing our lifesavers. We, we . . .*' The boy was cuffing his nose.

Wasim stopped punching in his bag and looked up. The boy said a swear word and brushed an arm across his eyes. Wasim felt sorry for him. '*It said "Good luck", my note.*'

'*Oh,*' said the boy.

Wasim forgot about his shirt and started pulling on his trousers which he'd found under the bench. He looked up. '*Do you want these?*' His trunks were still dry.

The boy sniffed again, '*No, you're alright. They'll all be out in a minute.*'

Wasim pulled his trousers up over his trunks and sat down again.

'*Here . . .*' The boy was up again. '*Have a laugh. Don't tell no one, eh?*' The boy had gone over to a big metal door, the warm door where Wasim liked to get a hook. '*We always go in here when no one's around. Come on.*'

The door was opened and Wasim was hit by a great balloon of heat. '*Come on, it's a grin.*'

Wasim didn't move.

'*Come on. What are they going to do, chuck you out?*' The boy disappeared and Wasim got up. Then he sat down. The boy's head popped back. '*Come on.*'

This would mean trouble. Wasim looked at the steps leading up to the poolside and heard the shouts of everyone having fun. And then he heard some clapping. He knew what that was for. Yeah, what could they do, chuck him out? This would mean real trouble, but somehow he was heading towards the darkness and the heat.

'*Shut the door.*'

Wasim couldn't see anything. He could just feel the warmth and hear a great humming noise.

'*It's the boiler. It heats up the water.*'

Things were getting clearer and Wasim could make out a blue light where the voice was coming from.

'*Come on over here, quick.*'

Wasim put his hands out like a tightrope walker

and edged past the shadowy heat of three huge shuddering machines.

'*This is it. Look. Like portholes. That's the pool.*'

Wasim reached the boy and the blue light. Yes, they were portholes, two of them, like windows on a ship, and that was the pool. He was looking through a window into the deep end. Underwater.

'*Look at his mug!*' The boy laughed and suddenly Wasim was laughing too. He was roaring. Through the window he could see Ben Perry trying to get something, a brick, off the bottom of the pool. But what a face he was pulling and yuk, there was stuff coming out of his nose! Wait till Wasim got back to school and told everybody that. He'd tell them when they were all eating, that'd show Ben up. Wasim laughed again and looked through the other porthole. Someone's legs were coming down the steps right next to the window. The legs started moving and Wasim lost sight of them in the thick blue glass. That would be someone doing their One Star.

Wasim's smile died, but the boy was pulling him back to the top window and Wasim could see why. Here was Ben again, going for the brick and this time his trunks were coming off and he was trying to pull them up and get the brick all at the same time. The High School boy was curled up with laughter. Wasim hugged himself, they'd never believe this.

'*What's your name?*' Wasim would have to know for when he told them.

'*Titch, Titch Jarvis.*' The boy sort of laughed but Wasim didn't know whether to or not. Maybe it was

189

only in his school that you had to call people by their proper names.

He went back to the other window. Some more legs were coming down the steps . . . slowly, very slowly. And there were trunks, so it was a boy. The legs started kicking, and there was . . . And there was Eric, legs kicking, arms clawing, face screaming and reaching, silently reaching up to the air and sinking past Wasim's glass. But Wasim had gone.

He sped through the darkness, letting the burns from the huge machines on his bare sides guide him back to the chinks of light where the door was. He crashed it open, ran through the changing room, made a mini-tidal wave in the foot-bath and slipped on the steps. He hardly had a breath left but he pulled himself up by the hand rail and finally reached the poolside. Which way? He headed for the steps – he'd know where they were in his sleep – and banged straight into a hard body. It was John, herding his group back to the changing rooms.

'*What?*'

'*Miss, Mm . . .*' Wasim knew nothing would come out, so he dragged John's shirt and turned him to face the steps at the deep end where Carol, her back to the water, was chatting to her lifeguard friend.

John looked down at him. Wasim pointed again and this time John was off, moving like a bullet along the side and into the water without a splash.

There was a second, a silent second, two, three, and then there was a huge bubble and one . . . two heads came out of the water. Still there was silence and then a wail, a huge wail from Eric.

Wasim realised that he had been holding his own breath too. He took in a great lungful of air and let out a wail of his own.

CHAPTER SIX

He wasn't very good at looking as if he didn't care. Wasim cared about everything he did. Sometimes that led to praise for hard work, like with his reading, and sometimes it led to arguments, like when he was playing football in the playground or when he moaned at somebody on his table for losing a group point. And now, in Friday assembly with his mum sitting at the back with all the other mums and dads, it meant that he couldn't sit still and laugh and clap with the others when Mr. Abbott handed over a white certificate and said, '*Andrew Foster, you are a star.*' It wasn't very funny really anyway.

What was worse was that he could feel as many eyes on him as on the lucky things out at the front. Everyone knew what had happened on Monday. They'd talked about it all week and up until today it had felt good. But today there was no getting away from it – whatever else he had done, he had not swum that twenty-five metres from the deep steps to the shallow steps.

Nicola was next up and Wasim slowly forced himself to clap. Then he saw Miss looking and clapped a bit faster. He looked round for Donna and Jamila. They were the only other two who hadn't got a certificate. They were clapping like anything and Wasim forced his hands together again while he sneaked a look at the clock. Topic time next, then break.

'*And now, boys and girls, we've got one more star.*'

Wasim jerked up. Donna hadn't done it, had she?

But Mr. Abbott wasn't talking about swimming; he was talking about something else, rules again. Wasim began cleaning the crack between two floor tiles while Mr. Abbott went on about something to do with the school rule about calling people by their own names. Something about a boy who had come from another country and who had been so worried that nobody would say his name properly that he had chosen a footballer's name, a United player's name. There was a buzz and Wasim stopped picking at the crack. '*Just,*' Mr. Abbott whispered in his very quietest specially for infants voice, '*to make it easy for people to say.*'

Heads twizzled everywhere. Who was it? Mr. Abbott waited until they settled down.

'*But,*' he told them finally, '*the boy had found a really good friend, a friend who was willing to give up things, very important things, like a special certificate, to help him. And because of this friend, the new boy trusted everybody at the school to be just as kind. So from now on,*' Mr. Abbott was walking down the middle and smiling, '*we are all going to call Eric by his proper name – Wing Ho.*'

They all swung round to where Junior S were sitting and everybody in the hall tried saying it . . .

'*Wing Ho.*' It wasn't that hard and Eric, Wing Ho, was beaming from ear to ear.

Then Mr. Abbott called for quiet again and said, '*I reckon a friend such as Wing Ho has found is a very special friend, don't you?*'

They all said yes.

'*Let's give him a big cheer then, shall we. Come up here, Wasim Ahmed.*

You really are a star.'

All that had happened an hour before. The rest of his class were doing their Vikings work now but Wasim had a tight grip on the rail, his foot on the first rough plastic step, and he was staring down through the shimmering water to see how deep 1.5 metres actually was.

It was deep. What if he didn't make it? Mr. Abbott had driven him and Wing Ho to the High School and then on to the baths in his Mondeo. He was missing a meeting just to give Wasim a chance of his One Star.

'*OK, Wasim? Take your time.*' It was John with the pole. There was no sign of Carol but there was a new lady on the other side doing a lifesaving test with Peter Jarvis.

Wasim looked down again. What if he didn't make it? He gripped the rail harder, had one last look along the pool and there, right down there by the other steps was Eric. No, not Eric, Wing Ho, and Wing Ho was shouting and clapping.

So what if he didn't make it. Wasim was already a

star. He let go. Twenty-five metres, he thought, and no armbands.

FOLLOW THAT BUS!

Pat Hutchins

1

RARING TO GO

The children of Class 6 peered anxiously out of the windows of the school bus as the church clock struck nine.

'There she goes!' said Mr. Coatsworth cheerfully. 'At least we've got the old girl started, and now if we give her a little chance to warm up while we're waiting for Miss Beaver, she should go like a bird.'

'I bet she doesn't come,' said Avril mournfully.

'I bet she's been run over or something.'

'Or kidnapped!' exclaimed Jessica dramatically. 'I saw a programme on TV once where a teacher was kidnapped. She was just walking quietly to school one day, when suddenly, out of nowhere, this big black car pulled up with a squeal of brakes . . . and then . . .'

'Perhaps she was eaten by a tiger,' Akbar interrupted, knowing how long Jessica's stories took. 'Tigers sometimes eat teachers in India.'

'But we're not in India,' said Dominic. 'We're in Hampstead. And there aren't any tigers in Hampstead.'

'I think she's forgotten.' Morgan sighed. 'Miss Beaver is always forgetting things,' he added, as Jessica staggered past him, acting out the kidnapping with bloodcurdling sound effects.

'Yoo-hoo!' The familiar voice cut short Jessica's imitation of a police siren.

'Here she comes!' Morgan shouted.

'Thank goodness she's safe,' said Jessica, pressing her nose to the window as Miss Beaver raced down the hill toward them, waving a lunch box in the air.

'Good morning, children,' said Miss Beaver as she staggered onto the bus and collapsed onto the front seat. 'I'm sorry I'm late, but I left my sandwiches on the 24 bus.'

'I told you,' whispered Morgan, nudging Dominic, who was sitting next to him.

'But I managed to catch up with the bus at Hampstead Hill bookshop and retrieve them,' she added, holding the lunch box up triumphantly.

'Now let me see,' she continued. 'I'm sure there's something I ought to do before we set off to the farm.'

'Count us,' said Avril.

'Of course!' exclaimed Miss Beaver. 'Thank you, Avril. Now let me see, there should be twenty of you.'

'Or kidnapped,' Jessica interrupted. 'I saw a programme on TV once about some children who were kidnapped.'

'Did you, dear?' Miss Beaver said hastily. 'That's

nice. You must tell us about it one day.' She started to count rapidly.

'One, two, three . . .'

'It was like this,' said Jessica, jumping down from her seat again.

'Six, seven, eight . . .' Miss Beaver paused, as Jessica screamed, clutched her side, and fell flat on her face in the aisle.

'Jessica,' said Miss Beaver gently, 'I wonder if you would mind sitting down, dear. I keep counting you twice.

'Eighteen, nineteen, twenty,' Miss Beaver finished. 'Good. Now you've all remembered your raincoats and sandwiches?'

'Yes, Miss,' chorused Class 6.

'In that case,' said Miss Beaver, smiling at Mr. Coatsworth, 'I think we can go.'

'Where to, Miss?' asked Mr. Coatsworth.

'Why, to the farm of course!' said Miss Beaver brightly. 'We don't want to keep Mr. and Mrs. Ramsbottom waiting. Oh dear!' she added, striking her forehead with her hand. 'How silly of me! I haven't given you the address. It's written on the maps in my holdall.' She started searching the floor of the bus.

'I had a copy made especially for you in case mine got mislaid, and I put both of them in the holdall. Now where did I put it?' she murmured, as the children at the front of the bus got onto their hands and knees and joined in the search.

'Please, Miss,' said Morgan, 'I don't think you had a holdall.'

'Oh, but I did, Morgan dear,' Miss Beaver said. 'I put my raincoat, my handbag, my lunch box, and the maps in it. In fact I distinctly remember taking my lunch box out so I could get at my purse for the bus fare.'

'I didn't see you bring it on the bus either, Miss,' said Avril. 'Someone must have pinched it!'

'Perhaps it was a spy,' said Jessica, 'trying to get secret information about a deadly new substance that turns people invisible.'

'Don't be silly,' said Dominic. 'What would a spy want with a raincoat, a handbag, and two roadmaps?'

'Maybe you left it on the bus,' Morgan suggested.

'The bus!' Miss Beaver cried. 'The bus!' she repeated. 'That's where I left it. Oh dear,' she said, turning to Mr. Coatsworth, 'what can we do? We can't go to the farm without the maps – they have the address on them.'

'Well,' said Mr. Coatsworth, patting the steering wheel, 'the old girl's raring to go – the 24 bus can't have reached Camden Town yet, so let's see if we can get them back.'

And as the school bus bounced forward in pursuit of the 24 bus, two desperate robbers were holding the staff of Barclays Bank in Camden Town at gunpoint, while the terrified clerks stuffed thousands of used banknotes into their black holdalls.

2

FOLLOW THAT BUS!

'Look, Miss, there it is,' Akbar shouted, 'just in front of us, the 24 bus.'

The rest of the class crowded to the front of the bus to look. 'It is, it is,' cried Jessica, 'and it's stopping at the bus stop!'

'Oh good!' exclaimed Miss Beaver, as Mr. Coatsworth pulled in behind it.

'Shan't be a moment,' she called, jumping off the school bus.

'I don't know why she's bothering,' said Avril glumly. 'Someone's bound to have pinched it.'

'She's gone through the wrong door,' said Morgan, as the automatic doors opened on the 24 bus and Miss Beaver leaped on, passing the solitary passenger who was getting off.

'Oh goodness!' Jessica squealed, as the doors closed and the bus drove off again. 'The driver's kidnapped our teacher!'

'Don't be silly,' said Dominic, as Jessica ran up and down the aisle waving her arms and shouting. 'He hasn't even seen her.'

'Don't worry!' said Mr. Coatsworth cheerfully. 'She'll have to get off at the next stop, it's the terminal.'

They could see Miss Beaver through the window – she'd found the holdall, and with a pleased smile on her face she took out one of the maps and pressed the button for the next stop.

The driver, who thought he had an empty bus, was so surprised he slammed the brakes on in an emergency stop.

'Aha!' exclaimed Mr. Coatsworth, slamming his brakes on too. The school bus screeched to a standstill.

'Crikey!' Dominic yelled, pointing to the back of the bus. 'Look!'

The rest of the class stared openmouthed out of the back window. Heading straight toward them was a big, powerful car, and behind it, with blue lights flashing and sirens screaming, were two police cars.

'Quick!' shouted Morgan. 'The floor!'

The whole class threw themselves flat on the floor. There was a tremendous crash. The bus juddered from the impact as the big car rammed into the back of the bus, and the two police cars rammed into the back of the big car.

The children lay still for a moment, then jumped up and raced to the back windows of the bus just as two masked men, clutching black holdalls and waving guns in the air, leaped out of the squashed car.

'Quick, Bert, the bus!' one of them shouted.

'Not that old banger, you fool!' he snarled, as Bert rattled the door handle of the school bus.

'That one!' He jerked his head toward the 24 bus.

The children watched in amazement as the doors of the 24 bus opened and Miss Beaver, who had explained all about the holdall to the driver and was stepping happily out, collided with Bert and fell backward into the bus again.

The doors closed, and before the police had even scrambled out of their wrecked cars, the bus roared off, with the driver, the two robbers, and Miss Beaver on board.

'Well!' said Mr. Coatsworth, when he realized what had happened. 'It takes more than a little kick up the backside to upset this old girl.' He threw the bus into gear.

'What do you say, kids?'

'Follow that bus!' screamed Class 6, just as the bus door opened and four dishevelled policemen clambered on.

'You took the very words out of my mouth,' said Sergeant Pattison grimly. Then the school bus, with a big dent in the back, leaped forward, jumped the traffic lights, and tore down the hill after the hijacked 24 bus.

3

THE GETAWAY

Mr. Coatsworth had the headlights full on and his hand pressed hard on the horn as he crouched over the steering wheel like a racing driver.

The children screamed for him to go faster, and the policemen hung out of the door, shouting at cars and pedestrians to get out of the way.

But Mr. Coatsworth had his foot jammed down as far as it would go on the accelerator, and the old bus was beginning to shake with the strain.

'They're getting away!' Jessica yelled, as the 24 bus receded into the distance.

'There's too much traffic!' Morgan shouted. A car roared toward them, and Mr. Coatsworth swerved in behind a lorry to avoid hitting it.

'I knew we wouldn't get to the farm,' Avril complained. 'I've never been to a farm before,' she added bitterly, as the 24 bus vanished over the rim of a hill.

'Oh no!' groaned the children, for not only had the bus disappeared, but holding up the traffic at the crossroads was an enormous articulated lorry.

Mr. Coatsworth ground the school bus to a halt,

and mopped his face while the children hopped up and down impatiently.

The policemen waved wildly for the lorry to move on, but the driver just shrugged and pointed to the line of cars in front of him.

'We'll never catch up with them now.' Dominic sighed, as the lorry inched its way slowly across their path.

'Poor Miss Beaver,' Jessica said, 'she was my most favourite teacher EVER!'

By the time the path was clear and the bus had roared off again, half the smaller children in the class had burst into tears at Jessica's vivid description of the dreadful things she thought would happen to their teacher in the hands of two desperate robbers.

They followed the road that the 24 bus had taken, but could see no sign of it.

'It's no good,' said Mr. Coatsworth, as they dropped over the hill where they'd last seen it. 'We might as well stop, they must be miles away by now.'

'Wait a minute!' said Morgan excitedly, running up to the front window. 'I think I can see something.'

'I can't,' said Sergeant Pattison, squinting into the distance.

'Neither can we,' said the other policemen.

'I'm sure I can,' said Morgan, who had eyes like a hawk. 'Look! Pulled off the road ahead.'

The rest of the class ran to the front of the bus to look, but they couldn't see anything either.

'By George!' said Sergeant Pattison, grabbing Mr. Coatsworth's arm and making the bus swerve.

'I believe the boy's right. Well done, lad!' he shouted. A small red dot appeared in the distance and gradually got bigger as the bus advanced toward it.

'It's the bus! It's the bus!' screamed the children.

'Why has it stopped?' asked Dominic.

'We'll soon find out,' said Mr. Coatsworth grimly, coaxing the bus to go even faster.

'There's Miss Beaver!' Morgan cried, as they got nearer the 24 bus. 'She's safe!'

'And the driver too,' shouted Akbar.

They shivered to a stop behind the 24 bus.

The children scrambled off the bus, tripping up the policemen who were trying to get off as well.

'Are you all right, Miss?' asked Sergeant Pattison, picking himself up and dusting his uniform down.

'Oh perfectly!' exclaimed Miss Beaver, her face pink with excitement as the children surrounded her, all talking at once.

'And you, sir?' he asked the driver, who was sitting on the grass looking slightly dazed. The driver nodded gloomily. 'We ran out of petrol,' he muttered. 'They went that way,' he added, pointing across the fields, 'and they took the money with them.'

'Right!' said Sergeant Pattison briskly. 'Smith and Pike, you come with me. Turner, I want you to find a telephone and call for help.' Then he leaped over the fence and disappeared across the fields.

And while Miss Beaver made a statement for the police, Mr. Coatsworth opened the bonnet to let the engine cool down, and poured some hot, sweet tea out of his thermos for the driver, who was still looking a bit stunned by it all.

'Well, children,' said Miss Beaver, after she'd answered all the policeman's questions and the driver had been taken back to the bus terminal in one of the police cars that had arrived.

'I've got my holdall back' – she patted the black holdall in her hand – 'and we have the map.' She waved the map she'd been clutching in the air. 'So let's go to the farm.'

'About time too,' Avril muttered.

'Oh!' moaned the rest of the class, who were all for following the sergeant across the fields.

'What a coincidence!' exclaimed Mr. Coatsworth, taking the piece of paper and looking at it. 'We've been following the route to the farm all along. It's only a mile or so from here,' he added, snapping the bonnet of the bus shut. 'We'll be there in no time!'

'I wish we'd found the robbers,' Morgan whispered to Dominic as they climbed onto the bus again.

'I don't,' announced Miss Beaver, who had overheard him. 'I think we've had quite enough excitement for one day,' she finished, closing the bus door.

MEADOW FARM

'We must be quite near the farm now,' said Miss Beaver, looking at the map as the bus bumped over a railroad crossing. 'It's very close to the station.

'Just think, children,' she added, although none of the children, except Avril, seemed terribly interested in visiting the farm now. They were talking excitedly about the robbery and the bus chase. 'Just think!' she repeated, raising her voice above the chatter. 'We might see some cows being milked if we're lucky.'

'Or a bull,' said Avril. 'I've never seen a bull before.'

'They don't milk bulls,' said Dominic flatly, thinking, like the rest of the class, how he'd much rather be chasing robbers across fields than watching cows being milked.

'I know that!' said Avril scornfully. 'I know all about bulls. Me dad told me how they could toss a man in the air, catch him on their horns, then trample him to death.'

'Oooh!' whispered Jessica, suddenly becoming interested in visiting the farm again. 'How AWFUL!

I read a story once about a great big bull, with absolutely ENORMOUS horns, and one day . . .'

'Left here, Mr. Coatsworth,' Miss Beaver interrupted hastily, as the bus reached a crossroads.

'I don't suppose they'll have a bull anyway.' Avril sighed.

Mr. Coatsworth swung the bus into a narrow lane, making Jessica, who had spotted an openmouthed audience of younger children at the back of the bus and was on her way to finish the story, stumble and fall onto her hands and knees.

'Are you all right, Jessica dear?' Miss Beaver asked anxiously.

'Of course, Miss,' said Jessica stiffly, still eyeing her audience from the floor. Then holding her hands up to her head like horns, she bellowed loudly to the wide-eyed children before standing up, dusting herself down, and walking with great dignity back to her seat.

'I was just being a bull,' she said, 'that's all.'

Miss Beaver waited until Jessica was safely seated before studying her map again.

'According to the map,' she said, 'we should be almost there.'

'There it is, Miss,' said Morgan, pointing into the distance where he could see a sign with MEADOW FARM written on it.

'I wish we didn't have to go,' he added wistfully. 'I wish we could have gone with the sergeant instead.'

'So do we, Miss,' shouted the rest of Class 6 (except for Avril, who had her nose pressed to the window, scanning the countryside anxiously for any sign of a ferocious bull).

'Well, you never know!' Mr. Coatsworth laughed, as the bus turned into the driveway of the farm. 'They might even be lurking around here, someplace.'

'Oh dear!' said Miss Beaver in alarm. 'I hope not! Anyway,' she added nervously, 'I'm sure the police will have caught them by now.'

'Just joking, Miss,' said Mr. Coatsworth, stopping the bus in front of the farmhouse.

'Although I must admit,' he added, chuckling and slapping the steering wheel, 'I've not enjoyed myself so much for donkeys' years.'

'We'll keep our eyes open,' Morgan hissed in his ear, as Miss Beaver opened the door, 'just in case.'

'Is this it?' demanded Avril, when all the children were off the bus. She paused to look at the ramshackle barn, the chicken coop, and the pig pen with three sleepy pigs in it. 'It's very small,' she said darkly, 'and I can't see no bull.'

'I can see two, I can see two!' screamed Jessica, tugging at the teacher's arm and pointing to a field.

'They're cows,' said Dominic. One of them bent its head, blinked its velvety eyes, and lowed gently at them.

'Are you sure?' whispered Jessica, grabbing hold of Miss Beaver's hand. 'They look like bulls to me!'

'Ah well,' Morgan murmured, as Jessica darted among the children, arguing about the difference between cows and bulls. 'At least they've got a tractor and trailer,' Morgan said. He brightened up a bit as he nudged Dominic. 'They might give us a ride on it if we ask.'

'Now then, children, calm down,' said Miss Beaver briskly. Jessica had somehow managed (without going herself) to coax a group of confused and nervous children to approach the fence and study the two animals to prove they were really and truly cows.

'You've all got your raincoats and sandwiches, haven't you?' Miss Beaver looked at her watch.

'After we've introduced ourselves to Mr. and Mrs. – ' she fumbled in her pocket for the map – 'Ramsbottom,' she read. 'We'll look round the farm, then have a little picnic in the field.'

The smaller children looked uncertainly at the cows.

'That field,' said Miss Beaver, pointing to the next field, which didn't have any animals in it, as she wasn't too sure about cows either.

'I'll tinker about with the old bus while you're looking round,' said Mr. Coatsworth. 'She had a bit of a rough ride this morning, poor old girl.'

'Here, Miss,' he added, handing Miss Beaver her holdall. 'Don't forget your bag. You know what happened last time you left it on a bus,' he said laughingly.

'Can I carry your bag, Miss?' asked Avril. 'As there ain't no bull?'

'Of course, Avril dear,' said Miss Beaver, handing the holdall to Avril.

'Look, Miss,' said Akbar, as the farmhouse door creaked open, 'there's the farmer and his wife.'

'Come on, children,' said Miss Beaver gaily. 'Let's go and meet them.'

And as she marched up to the farmhouse, with the children straggling halfheartedly behind, Miss Beaver had to admit to herself that never, in all her life, had she seen anyone as remarkably ugly as the farmer.

Excepting, perhaps, his unfortunate wife.

5

MR. AND MRS. RAMSBOTTOM

The children stared at the couple in amazement.

They could hardly believe their eyes.

The farmer was ugly enough, with his tiny, close-set eyes and his squashed nose, and the hideous scars that ran across his face from one cauliflower ear to the other.

But his wife! She was incredible!!! She was dressed in what looked like a long nightdress and wellingtons. The scarf she had wrapped round her huge head and tied under her enormous chin managed to conceal some of the face. But the bit that showed was astonishing.

Her face was so thick with powder she looked as if someone had tipped a bag of flour over her head and she'd forgotten to blow afterward. Her stubby eyelashes were white, her thick bushy eyebrows were white, and even the rims of her watery eyes were white. And somewhere near the bottom of the whiteness was a gash of brilliant red lipstick, which covered the whole of her mouth and most of her chin. She had a broken nose, and when she smiled coyly at them, her front two teeth were missing.

'Blimey!' whispered Avril, instinctively taking a step backward with the rest of the class.

'Hello,' said Miss Beaver bravely, holding her hand out hesitantly to the farmer. 'You must be – ' she fumbled for the map again and looked at it – 'Mr. Ramsbottom.'

'Yeah,' said the farmer, nudging his wife, 'Ramsbottom. That's our name.'

'And you must be Mrs. Ramsbottom,' Miss Beaver added, offering her hand to the farmer's wife, as the farmer had ignored it.

The farmer's wife grunted and shuffled her feet.

'She don't say much,' the farmer said, tapping his forehead and nudging his wife again. 'On account of she's got a few screws loose.'

'Oh!' said Miss Beaver, startled by the farmer's bluntness. 'I'm Miss Beaver from New End School,' she added nervously, 'and this is Class 6.'

'Wotcher!' the farmer said, glancing furtively at the children. His eyes rested on Avril, who was clutching the teacher's holdall tightly, mesmerized by the farmer's wife.

''Ere,' he said, taking a step toward her. 'What's a little tiddler like you doing heaving a great heavy bag like that around for?'

He bent down and looked into Avril's eyes.

'I'll carry it for you,' he said coaxingly.

Avril gripped the handle even tighter.

'You ain't got no bull,' she said accusingly.

'What?' said the farmer, stepping back in surprise. Miss Beaver laughed uncertainly.

'I'm afraid Avril was rather disappointed that you didn't have a bull,' she explained, 'so I said she could carry my bag. It isn't heavy,' she added. 'It only has my handbag and raincoat in it.'

'Well, I wouldn't want you to think I wasn't no gentleman, now, would I?' said the farmer, gritting his yellow teeth into a grin, and tugging at the bottom of the holdall.

Avril put both arms round the bag and pulled back, staring defiantly at the farmer, whose grin was fading rapidly.

'I expect she'll get tired of carrying it soon,' Miss Beaver said hastily, not wanting to hurt the farmer's feelings.

The farmer muttered to himself and let go suddenly. 'Yeah!' he said, scowling, as Avril fell backward. 'She'd better – I mean I'd feel better,' he added quickly, helping an indignant Avril to her feet, 'carrying it myself.'

He lowered his voice and clasped his hands together tightly. 'You see, I just love children. And it breaks my heart to think of the poor little things going and straining themselves, like. You know what I mean?'

Miss Beaver nodded politely, although she didn't know what he meant at all.

The children had begun whispering amongst themselves, and Miss Beaver, not wanting the farmer and his wife to overhear them, said very loudly, 'It was awfully kind of you to offer to show us round the farm, but I'm sure we can manage on our own, can't we, children?' She turned desperately to the children who were whispering even louder now, and she was sure she heard Jessica murmur 'Frankenstein' in Akbar's ear.

'YOU MUST BE TERRIBLY BUSY!' she shouted at the farmer, trying to drown the children's conversation.

'No, we ain't,' said the farmer. 'We ain't got nothing to do but show you round, have we, Missus?' He dug his elbow into his wife, who didn't seem to hear him as she stared foolishly at the ground.

'HAVE WE, MISSUS?' he repeated, clipping his wife smartly round the ear.

'Hey. Watch it!' his wife replied in a gruff, reproachful voice.

'Just a little playful larking about,' said the farmer, laughing as he raised his fist and thumped his wife violently between the shoulder blades.

'The poor old girl's got a touch of laryngitis, ain't yer?' he roared in her ear.

His wife nodded slowly, then lifting her muscular arm, sent the farmer flying with a return clout.

The farmer staggered to his feet and advanced menacingly toward his wife.

The children held their breath, waiting for the blow to fall. But the farmer, instead of hitting her, tweaked his wife playfully on the cheek.

'As I was saying,' he said cheerfully to Miss Beaver, who was beginning to look a bit alarmed, 'just a little playful larking about. Now,' he added, glancing slyly at the breathless children, and nudging his wife yet again, 'to show these little darlings around.'

Dominic prodded Morgan, who had edged his way to the front of the class.

'Please, sir,' said Morgan politely, 'you haven't seen two masked men around, have you? There was a robbery and we chased them, but they got away.'

'Masked men?' the farmer repeated vaguely. 'We ain't seen no masked men, have we, Missus?' He thrust his face close to his wife's.

His wife shook her head vigorously.

'We ain't seen nothing,' she squeaked in a falsetto voice.

Goodness, thought Miss Beaver, her laryngitis has cleared up quickly.

'Oh!' said Morgan, disappointed.

Dominic nudged Morgan again.

'Then please could we have a ride on your tractor?' he added quickly.

'Please, Miss, I'm starving to death,' Jessica complained. 'Can't we have our picnic first?'

'I don't want to ride on no tractor,' Avril said. 'I want to look around the farm.'

'We want a ride on the tractor too, Miss,' the rest of Class 6 chorused.

'Well,' said the farmer, stroking his chin thoughtfully. 'I think I can keep you all happy, you know what I mean? The missus here can show Avril round the farm' – he patted Avril gently on the cheek, and winked slowly at his wife – 'while I give the rest of

219

you kids a quick turn on the tractor before you has your nosh.'

Avril looked at the wife doubtfully, but finally muttered, 'All right.' The rest of the class, led by Miss Beaver, followed the farmer across to the tractor and trailer.

As Avril, still clutching the holdall tightly, went into the barn with the farmer's wife, she noticed, with surprise, a faint stubble of whiskers protruding through the thick white powder on Mrs. Ramsbottom's face.

THE ROBBERS!

The children waited impatiently while the farmer, glancing furtively over his shoulder toward the barn all the time, fiddled with the knobs on the tractor.

'I don't think he knows how to drive it,' Morgan whispered to Dominic. The farmer pressed every button and tapped every dial on the dashboard, but still couldn't get the engine started.

'Please, sir,' said one of the littler children, who was still not sure about the cows in the field. 'Are they cows or bulls over there?'

'Is what cows or bulls?' asked the farmer, looking around vaguely.

'There!' said Jessica, stabbing her finger at the field. The farmer looked confused for a moment, then catching Dominic's eye, said, 'You look like a smart lad, tell her what they are.'

'Cows!' said Dominic proudly.

'Yeah!' said the farmer. 'Cows. That's what they are.'

'And what breed are the pigs?' Miss Beaver asked politely, as the farmer started kicking the tractor angrily, still peering anxiously in the direction of the barn.

'Pigs,' said the farmer, 'what pigs?'

'Why those,' said Miss Beaver, glancing at the three sleepy pigs. The farmer looked at the pigs in desperation.

'Let's see,' he said, stroking his chin. 'Any smart kid know what breed these pigs is?'

Class 6 shook their heads.

The farmer looked relieved. 'They're longhorns, ain't they?' he said.

'Please, sir,' said Jessica, 'I thought longhorns were cattle. I saw a film once, where a cowboy was trampled to death by longhorns . . .'

'Aha,' interrupted the farmer, scowling at Jessica, 'just trying to catch you out. You know what I mean?'

'They're shorthorns,' he added fiercely, thrusting his face toward Jessica's.

Jessica stepped back nervously, then the farmer's scowl changed to an oily smile.

'Sharp as a razor blade, this 'un,' he said to Miss Beaver, patting Jessica gently on her cheek.

The children were beginning to feel very hungry as they stood watching the farmer kicking the tractor and jerking his head toward the barn between each kick, and were quite relieved when Mr. Coatsworth stuck his head out of the bus and shouted, 'You forgot your lunch, Miss,' and jumped down from the bus to join them, carrying Miss Beaver's sandwiches and his own packed lunch.

'Please, Miss,' said Jessica, clutching her stomach. 'I'm absolutely dying of starvation. I can't go another minute,' she added dramatically, 'without food.'

'Neither can we, Miss,' said the rest of the class, realizing that the chances of a ride on the tractor were getting very slim.

'Here!' Mr. Coatsworth laughed and pulled a large bag of sweets from his pocket. 'Have an aniseed ball to keep you going.'

The children lost interest in the farmer when they saw the bag, and crowded round Mr. Coatsworth as he handed out the sweets.

The farmer had lost interest in the children too, and was staring openly at the barn.

'I think,' said Miss Beaver, 'that if you don't mind we'd better have our picnic now.' She glanced at her watch. 'It's getting rather close to lunch time.'

'Yeah!' muttered the farmer, shading his eyes and staring past her. 'The old geezer don't seem to want to go anyway.' His eyes suddenly lit up, as he caught a glimpse of his wife, lurking by the side of the house and beckoning furiously to him.

'I'm feeling a bit peckish myself,' he said slowly. 'I think I'll go and get some grub too.'

Mr. Coatsworth offered him an aniseed ball. 'Ta!' he said, grabbing a huge handful and stuffing them in his pocket. Then strolling casually toward the farm-house, he threw one high in the air and caught it in his gaping mouth.

What a strange gentleman, Miss Beaver thought,

as she and Mr. Coatsworth followed the children to the empty field.

'Here's a good spot, Miss,' Akbar said, spreading his raincoat on the damp grass and sitting down.

Miss Beaver watched the rest of the children spreading their raincoats out too, thinking she would do the same, when she realized that hers was in the bag that Avril was carrying. She looked around, but couldn't see any sign of Avril.

'Has anyone seen Avril?' she asked.

'She went off with the farmer's wife,' said Akbar, 'to look round the farm.'

'That's funny,' said Morgan. 'I saw the farmer's wife go into the house, but Avril wasn't with her.'

'Oh dear,' said Miss Beaver. 'I do hope she hasn't got lost. I think perhaps we ought to go and look for her,' she added nervously.

'There she is!' Dominic shouted, as a dishevelled figure came tearing toward them, shouting at the top of its voice.

'Good heavens!' exclaimed Miss Beaver, grabbing Mr. Coatsworth's arm. 'Whatever is happening?'

For, not only was Avril shouting, but the bedroom window of the farmhouse had suddenly been thrown open, and two complete strangers, waving their arms wildly in the air, joined in the shouting too.

And in the distance, yelping dogs, whinnying horses, and huntsmen's horns added to the commotion.

'Look!' yelled Morgan above the din.

Two figures, clutching black holdalls, were running toward the bus.

'Oh no!' whispered Miss Beaver faintly, as one of them nearly tripped over his long skirt and threw the scarf (which had fallen over his eyes) to the ground, revealing a shaven head.

'It's the robbers!' screamed the children, jumping to their feet and chasing after Mr. Coatsworth, who was already racing after the two crooks.

But they were too late. The bus engine started up, and with Sid at the wheel and Bert clinging tightly onto the door, the bus swerved out of the farmyard and careered down the drive toward the open road.

'Quick, kids! Into the trailer!' shouted Mr. Coatsworth, jumping into the driving seat of the tractor. Avril and Miss Beaver caught up with the rest of the class and threw themselves into the trailer too.

And as the tractor's engine roared into life, they didn't even notice Sergeant Pattison and his men staggering wearily into the farmyard with a pack of snapping foxhounds at their heels, and the confused members of the County Hunt galloping behind them.

7

THE TRACTOR CHASE

The children were wild with excitement. They bounced and swayed in the trailer, shouting and screaming at Mr. Coatsworth, urging him to go faster as he desperately tried to catch up with the retreating bus.

'He locked me in the barn,' Avril kept yelling indignantly. 'When I said I thought he was really a bloke, he grabbed the bag and locked me in the barn.'

'But what on earth did he want with my bag?' Miss Beaver interrupted.

'And why were they pretending to be Mr. and Mrs. Ramsbottom?' asked Akbar.

'And how did they know we were going to the farm?' Dominic demanded.

'I still think they're spies,' said Jessica wildly, 'trying to get secret information about a deadly new substance that turns people invisible.'

Dominic sighed. 'I told you before,' he said. 'A raincoat, a handbag, and a roadmap aren't any use to a spy. Anyway,' he added, 'they're robbers, not spies.'

Morgan, who had been listening to the conversation with a funny look on his face, jumped up suddenly.

'That's it!' he shouted.

The children stopped screaming at Mr. Coatsworth and looked at him in astonishment.

'That's it!' he repeated, hanging onto the side of the trailer to steady himself. 'The map!'

'See!' said Jessica proudly. 'Morgan thinks they were after Miss Beaver's bag too!'

'But they didn't want Miss Beaver's bag!' Morgan cried. 'Don't you see?' He turned to Miss Beaver. 'Your holdall is exactly the same as the two they had. They must have got mixed up when they hijacked the 24 bus, and when they discovered the map in your bag, they knew we were going to the farm.'

'So they disguised themselves as Mr. and Mrs. Ramsbottom,' Dominic added slowly, 'to try and get their holdall back!'

'Then that strange couple at the window must be the real farmer and his wife!' gasped Miss Beaver.

'And I,' shrieked Avril, 'have been walking round all morning with half their loot!'

'Well,' Mr. Coatsworth shouted over his shoulder, 'they've got all of it now. And it looks like they'll get away with it too,' he added, as the bus pulled even farther away from them, and headed toward the level crossing.

'Look!' shouted Morgan, who had spotted a train in the distance and the stationmaster hurrying toward the gate to close it. 'They'll have to stop!'

But the robbers didn't stop. And the stationmaster, who had already started to close the gate, pulled it back in amazement as the bus roared through the gap, bounced safely over the track, and landed on the other side of the road.

'If they can do it,' Mr. Coatsworth yelled, jamming his foot hard on the accelerator, 'so can we!'

The stationmaster, who had started closing the gate again, saw the tractor and trailer heading toward him at full tilt, and leaping onto the gate, swung back, with his eyes tightly closed.

'Please, Miss,' Akbar shouted, as the express thundered toward them, 'I can hear dogs barking!'

But Miss Beaver and the rest of the children (who had their eyes tightly closed too) didn't hear him. The huge engine, missing them by inches, tore down the line behind them.

'Or I thought I could,' Akbar murmured to himself, glancing back at the engine and the long line of swaying coaches that rattled along the track.

The children opened their eyes again as the tractor and trailer turned a bend in the road.

Mr. Coatsworth braked suddenly, throwing the children on top of one another.

'Good heavens!' exclaimed Miss Beaver. 'It's stopped!'

Mr. Coatsworth jumped down from the tractor and looked suspiciously at the bus in the distance. It was parked at such an angle that, although they could see the rear of it, the door and driving cab were completely hidden by the curve in the road.

'We'd better be careful,' he murmured. 'It might be a trap. I think you kids had better stay here while we investigate.' He nodded to Miss Beaver, who nodded back weakly, wishing Mr. Coatsworth had said 'I' instead of 'we.'

'Remember, they have a gun,' Miss Beaver said nervously as the children complained.

'And if we get the bus back – I mean when – ' she added quickly, 'we're going straight back to the farm to have our lunch, robbers or no robbers.'

'Please, Miss,' said Jessica miserably, 'they may as well shoot me, I'm half dead from hunger already.'

'Here,' said Mr. Coatsworth, pulling the half-empty bag of sweets from his pocket. 'Share them out while you're waiting.'

And while the children sucked slowly on their aniseed balls, Miss Beaver and Mr. Coatsworth crept cautiously up the road toward the school bus, completely unaware of the village policeman cycling furiously toward it from the opposite direction.

A DREADFUL MISTAKE

'They're not in the bus,' whispered Mr. Coatsworth. He and Miss Beaver stood on tiptoe and pressed their noses against the bus window. 'They must have made off across the fields.'

'Look!' cried Miss Beaver, pointing to the corridor. 'They've dropped something.'

They clambered onto the bus to see what it was. Mr. Coatsworth whistled as he bent down and picked the object up.

'They certainly did drop something,' he said grimly, handing it carefully to Miss Beaver, who gazed at it in horror.

'Aha!' said a voice behind them.

Miss Beaver spun round in alarm, the gun falling from her hand.

'Oh!' she cried in relief, seeing the policeman dive to the floor to pick it up. 'Thank goodness!'

'So,' said the policeman, clutching the gun nervously. 'Saw me coming, eh? Frightened, eh?? Thought you'd do a little disappearing act, eh???'

'No!' said Miss Beaver in surprise.

'Oh!' said the policeman, shifting his feet awkwardly and looking a bit put out.

'Ready to cooperate then?' he added hopefully.

'Of course!' said Miss Beaver, smiling.

'And you, sir?' The policeman looked warily at Mr. Coatsworth.

'Certainly,' said Mr. Coatsworth.

'Good!' said the policeman. 'Hold out your hands.'

Mr. Coatsworth and Miss Beaver looked at each other in surprise, shrugged, and held their hands out.

'Hey!' shouted Mr. Coatsworth as the policeman snapped a pair of handcuffs onto one of his wrists.

'Goodness!' said Miss Beaver, looking down at her wrist, which was now firmly attached to Mr. Coatsworth.

'Ha!' said the policeman, wagging his finger at the astonished Miss Beaver. 'A good disguise. A very good disguise. Could fool a lot of people. But not me,' he finished proudly. 'Now. Where's the money?'

Miss Beaver looked at Mr. Coatsworth in alarm.

'What on earth is the man talking about?' she asked.

Mr. Coatsworth, who had been looking just as bewildered as Miss Beaver, suddenly slapped his leg with his free hand and burst out laughing. The policeman gripped the gun tightly in his hand and looked at him uneasily.

'So,' he said. 'Think we won't find it, eh? Hidden it under a seat, eh??' He waved the gun wildly round the bus. 'Or maybe in the luggage rack, eh???'

231

Mr. Coatsworth shook with laughter, tears rolling down his face.

'I'm sorry,' he gasped, looking at Miss Beaver's anxious face. He slapped his leg again to try and stifle his laughter.

'He thinks we're the robbers,' he spluttered, 'and that you're really a man!'

'Oh!' said Miss Beaver, not sure whether to laugh or not.

The policeman's eyes narrowed suspiciously. 'Now look here,' he said uncomfortably. 'You won't catch me out with any of your little games. I know exactly who you are. Sergeant Pattison telephoned me from the farm. Two fellows' – he jerked the gun at Mr. Coatsworth and then Miss Beaver – 'one dressed as a woman,' he added darkly, 'driving a bus.' He waved the gun around the bus again.

'And armed with a gun,' he finished, glancing down at the gun.

Miss Beaver laughed awkwardly. 'But you've made a dreadful mistake,' she protested. 'I am Miss Beaver from New End School, and this is Mr. Coatsworth, the school driver.'

'Oh yes!' said the policeman sarcastically. 'And I'm Napoleon.'

'Well, Constable Napoleon,' said Miss Beaver, shaking her wrist, 'perhaps you'll take these silly things off now. My children are very hungry and it's past their lunch time.'

'Yes,' said the policeman slowly, eyeing the empty bus.

'They look hungry, very hungry. In fact so hungry that they've faded away,' he added, laughing dryly at his own joke.

'The children,' Miss Beaver said coldly, 'are not in the bus.'

Mr. Coatsworth wiped his eyes with the back of his free hand. 'They're down the road a bit,' he said, trying not to laugh, 'in a trailer.'

'Down the road a bit, eh?' the policeman repeated. 'In a trailer, eh?? That's a good one!'

'Go and see for yourself if you don't believe us,' said Miss Beaver crossly.

'Ha!' said the policeman. 'You'd like that, eh? Get me off the bus, eh?? Drive off and leave me behind, eh???'

'Oh dear!' said Miss Beaver wearily. 'Then we'll come with you if you like.'

'That's better,' said the policeman, and with the gun still pointed at them, he backed out of the bus, lifted his bicycle into it, and closed the door behind him.

'And you'd better come quietly, mind,' he added. 'I've got the gun now, remember.'

'Good heavens!' said Miss Beaver weakly. 'The man's gone mad.'

And to Miss Beaver's and Mr. Coatsworth's astonishment, the policeman, who had never driven a car before in his life, let alone a bus, climbed into the driver's seat.

A DIRTY DOUBLECROSS

The children were beginning to get tired of waiting and climbed out of the trailer to stretch their legs.

'Do you think they've been shot?' Jessica whispered, popping another aniseed ball into her mouth. 'And that they're too weak to call for help?'

'No,' murmured Morgan, who was shading his eyes with his hand and squinting across the fields.

'We would have heard the explosion,' Dominic added, gazing at the back of the bus, trying in vain to see what was going on inside it.

'I bet the robbers have got them though,' said Avril bitterly. 'I bet they've tied them up and dumped them in the hedge and we'll never get back to the farm.'

'What about our lunch?' wailed the children. 'We're starving.'

'Perhaps we'll all starve to death,' said Jessica solemnly, 'and our bones won't be found for years, and years, and years . . .'

'Listen!' Akbar interrupted. 'I can hear those dogs again.'

'You don't think they're wolves, do you?' cried Jessica, grabbing his arm in alarm.

'I saw a TV programme once about a group of children who were slowly starving to death at the North Pole, and the wolves waited and waited until they were too weak to fight, and then . . .'

'Look!' screamed Avril, pointing to the bus. 'The bus! It's moving!'

'Oooh!' squealed Jessica. 'It's the robbers! They've kidnapped our teacher again!'

'Wait!' Morgan shouted, as the children started running after the bus. He waved his arms frantically in the direction of the field. 'It can't be the robbers! There they are!'

The children turned, to see two small figures disappearing over the top of a hill.

'Quick, after them!' yelled Morgan, climbing over the fence. The rest of the children ran back in confusion.

'Crikey!' gasped Akbar, glancing over his shoulder as he stumbled through the long grass after Morgan. 'We're being followed by a pack of hounds!'

Dominic looked over his shoulder too, and shook his head in disbelief.

For galloping wildly down the road after the school bus, clinging tightly to each other and the neck of the horse they had commandeered (and were sharing between them) were Sergeant Pattison and his men, hotly pursued by the members of the County Hunt in full cry, and Mr. and Mrs. Ramsbottom on an ancient tandem. But the dogs, instead of staying with the hunters, had sniffed the trailer, jumped the fence, and ignoring the huntsmen's angry cries, ran yapping and whining across the fields after the children.

'Help!' shrieked Jessica, as one of the hounds caught up with her, knocked her over, and started licking her face furiously. 'I'm being eaten alive!'

'So am I!' gasped Avril, as a bunch of dogs ran between her legs, tripped her up, and started licking her too.

'And me!'

'And me!' The shout echoed across the fields as one by one the children were knocked off their feet, and their faces licked clean by the excited hounds.

Morgan, who was well ahead of them and didn't hear the commotion, stopped suddenly in his tracks. For just in front of him, clutching a black holdall and desperately trying to free his long nightdress from a thorn bush, was Bert.

Morgan closed his eyes, took a deep breath, then lunged at Bert's feet, hanging on for grim death and shouting at the top of his voice, until the rest of the children, realizing that the dogs weren't going to eat them after all, scrambled to their feet and stumbled up the hill after him.

'Help, Sid, help!' Bert screamed, furiously shaking his foot to try and free it when he saw the rest of Class 6 and the pack of hounds heading toward him. But Sid, instead of going to his crony's aid, leaped over a hedge and ran off as fast as his legs would carry him, laughing maliciously.

Before Bert had time to open his mouth again the children leaped at him. His long nightdress tore free and he was pinned to the ground.

The hounds, beside themselves with excitement, leaped on him too, but after sniffing the bit of him that wasn't smothered by children, lost interest, and poked their wet noses into the children's pockets instead.

Morgan looked across the fields to where Sid had disappeared, and frowned.

'It's a pity he got away,' he murmured. 'Still,' he added, picking up the holdall that Bert had dropped, 'at least we've got half the money.'

'What are we going to do now?' Dominic asked, as the children bounced up and down on Bert's stomach. 'We can't sit on him forever!'

'Torture him,' said Avril grimly, twisting one of his ears. 'That's for locking me in the barn,' she muttered ferociously, 'and that' – she twisted his other ear – 'is for taking the bag.'

'Shout,' said Morgan. 'Someone's bound to hear us.'

'I wonder what happened to Miss Beaver and Mr. Coatsworth,' Akbar said, as the children shouted at the top of their lungs.

'There they are!' Jessica shrieked. 'Look!'

Hurrying across the fields toward them were Miss Beaver and Mr. Coatsworth, and limping behind them were Sergeant Pattison and his men (who had been thrown off the horse so many times, they'd decided it was safer to walk) and shuffling behind

237

them was the red-faced village policeman, and behind the village policeman were the farmer and his wife, and galloping up in the rear were the indignant members of the County Hunt.

'Look, everyone!' Avril shouted, snatching the holdall from Morgan and waving it in the air.

Bert lifted his head wearily to have one last look at his loot.

'Oh no!' cried the children in horror, for as Avril swung the bag, the catch broke and the holdall dropped open.

'The dirty double-crosser!' Bert snarled. A raincoat, a handbag, and a roadmap fell out.

10

ANISEED BALLS!

The children stared at the holdall silently, too disappointed even to bother to push away the hounds that were ferreting in their pockets and eating any aniseed balls they found there, while Miss Beaver, Mr. Coatsworth, Mr. and Mrs. Ramsbottom, the policemen, and the huntsmen crowded round them.

'I'm sorry we kept you waiting for so long, children,' Miss Beaver said breathlessly, 'but that, that' – she stabbed her finger at the local policeman, who blushed and stared at his boots.

'Policeman,' she said coldly, 'arrested us. He thought WE were the robbers. It's a good thing Sergeant Pattison and his men overtook us on their horse and flagged him down, or goodness knows what would have happened to us. He was driving the bus like a maniac . . .

'Oh my goodness!' she gasped, when she caught a glimpse of Bert's desperate face from under the pile of bodies. 'It's that woman – I mean man! Oh dear,' she added in concern, 'are you all right, children?'

The children nodded halfheartedly.

'They might be all right,' gasped Bert, 'but I ain't. They're knocking the stuffing out of me.'

'Serves you right!' snapped Mrs. Ramsbottom, who was circling him looking for a bit of flesh to get at, until Avril obligingly stood up, revealing a hairy arm where the nightdress had torn.

'I've a good mind to set Mr. Ramsbottom onto you,' she added, nipping his arm fiercely with her plump fingers and jerking her head toward her timid husband, who was grinning weakly and backing away from them.

'There, there,' said Sergeant Pattison soothingly, as Mrs. Ramsbottom raised her handbag above Bert's head. 'He'll get what's coming to him.'

She lowered her handbag reluctantly.

'What about that other fellow?' she demanded.

'He went that way,' said Morgan miserably, pointing across the fields, 'but we'll never catch him now, and he's got all the money.'

'Never mind, lad,' said Sergeant Pattison kindly, 'at least you've caught one of them, and we'll get the other one eventually, don't you worry.'

'And you did get my holdall back,' Miss Beaver added, trying to cheer them up a bit.

'What I want to know,' interrupted the leader of the hunt crossly, 'is what you children have done to our hounds. They've been going berserk since they got your scent!'

'Huh!' Avril snorted, trying unsuccessfully to push away a dog that was licking her. 'It ain't what we've been doing to your hounds. It's what your hounds have been doing to us!'

'They've been trying to eat us,' Jessica added indignantly, 'just like that TV programme where the wolves knew the children were starving to death and were too weak and hungry to fight back.'

'Haha!' muttered Bert mirthlessly, rubbing his smarting ears.

'Hey!' Akbar shouted, as a dog poked its nose into his pocket. 'It's taken my last aniseed ball!'

'And mine!' said Dominic.

'And mine!' the rest of the class shouted, feeling in their pockets.

'ANISEED BALLS!' the leader of the hunt thundered. 'You haven't been feeding them ANISEED BALLS!!'

'We didn't feed them no aniseed balls,' said Avril flatly. 'They stole them.'

'Aniseed balls,' the huntsman repeated, turning to the other riders, who threw their hands up in horror. 'Would you believe it?'

'Don't you realize,' he added fiercely, staring at Avril, 'that hounds will follow the trail of aniseed ANYWHERE?! No wonder they've been acting peculiar.'

'Well, they've eaten them all now,' said Avril, eyeing the dogs with a murderous look, as they sat happily munching the last of the sweets.

'And we're starving,' said Jessica accusingly.

'Well,' said Miss Beaver decisively, 'we're going back to the farm to finish our picnic now, if Mr. and

Mrs. – er . . .' she paused to pull the map out of her pocket, 'Ramsbottom,' she read, 'don't mind.'

The farmer grinned, quite relieved to have an excuse to get away. 'Not at all,' he said. 'I'm feeling a bit peckish myself.'

'How strange,' Miss Beaver murmured, frowning thoughtfully to herself, 'that's exactly what that dreadful man said the last time I suggested lunch; and Mr. Coatsworth here offered him an aniseed ball.'

'And the rogue took a handful,' added Mr. Coatsworth, shaking his head at the thought.

'AND STUFFED THEM IN HIS POCKET!' Morgan shouted, jumping up and staring at the hounds, who seemed to have lost interest in the children now that the sweets were gone, and were sniffing in the direction of the fields.

'And they said,' Sergeant Pattison murmured, glancing at the huntsman, 'that . . .'

'A HOUND WILL FOLLOW THE TRAIL OF ANISEED ANYWHERE!' screamed the children.

And before Miss Beaver had time to protest, the children were on their feet and tearing after the hounds, who had caught the scent of more aniseed and were yapping and barking excitedly as they bounded across the fields.

'Come on, men!' yelled Sergeant Pattison. 'Follow those hounds!' and leaving the bewildered village policeman to take care of Bert, he and his men chased after them, followed by Miss Beaver, Mr. Coatsworth, and Mrs. Ramsbottom, dragging her reluctant husband behind her.

'Yoicks! Tallyho!' shouted the leader of the hunt, not wanting to miss out on a chase, and with a blast on the horn, the County Hunt charged forward too.

11

CAPTURED

The children raced after the baying hounds, their legs aching and their hearts pounding.

'We're heading back toward the farm,' Akbar gasped, recognizing the farmyard in the distance.

'I can see our sandwiches,' said Jessica longingly.

'I bet we won't catch him,' Avril grumbled. 'I bet he's got away.'

'No, he hasn't,' Morgan yelled, spotting a tiny figure just in front of the pursuing hounds, heading toward a barred gate. 'There he is!'

'Out of the way, you,' shouted the huntsmen, who had galloped up behind them and overheard Morgan. 'This one's ours!'

And as the riders charged through the children, knocking them aside, Sid turned, saw the dogs, and clambered desperately over the gate.

'Blimey!' said Avril angrily, picking herself up as the policemen, Mr. Coatsworth, Miss Beaver, and the farmer and his wife caught up with them. 'That bunch ain't got no manners!' she fumed. The rest of the children jumped up too, and with a fresh burst of energy, ran toward the gate, just as the huntsmen disappeared over it.

'Goodness!' said Miss Beaver, as they all peered over the gate, for Sid had stopped suddenly in his tracks, turned, and with a cry of terror, zigzagged his way back past the men on horseback, with the dogs snapping at his heels.

'Oh! Look!' cried Avril in delight, seeing what had made Sid change direction. She opened the gate for him to stagger through. 'A BULL!'

And as the rest of the class, the dogs, the policemen, Mr. Coatsworth, Miss Beaver, and the farmer and his wife leaped on Sid, the huntsmen wheeled their horses round in alarm. The bull, pounding the earth with its hooves and snorting, was thundering toward them.

The riders shrieked in horror, then clinging tightly to the necks of the frightened horses, they galloped toward the gate that Avril (transfixed with joy at the sight of a bull) was still holding open. Jostling each other to get out of the way, they fought furiously to get through it as the angry bull pounded up behind them.

While the children watched in amazement, the bull charged first one, then another rider, scattering them in different directions until they had vanished completely.

'Oh!' Avril sighed. 'Isn't he WONDERFUL?'

'You naughty boy, Buttons,' said Mrs. Ramsbottom, letting go of Sid's nose as the bull snorted in satisfaction, then trotted meekly across to her.

'I can't think what came over him,' she added, stroking the beast's head and leading him back into the field.

'He's usually as gentle as a lamb,' she explained to the nervous children, closing the gate again. 'It must have been the red coats that upset him.'

In all the commotion, the dogs had managed to squeeze their way past the children to get at Sid's pockets. And having eaten all the aniseed balls, they wandered aimlessly across the fields.

'Well,' said Sergeant Pattison, after he'd snapped a pair of handcuffs onto Sid's wrists and picked up the two holdalls, 'I can't thank you children enough.' He beamed as he patted the two bags. 'There'll be a reward of course and I wouldn't be surprised if you weren't all National Heroes by tomorrow morning!'

'Well!' Miss Beaver said. 'If you don't mind, I think our National Heroes ought to have their lunch now.'

The children, Miss Beaver, and the farmer's wife took a short cut across the fields to the farm. Sergeant Pattison and his men took Sid to the police station, while Mr. Ramsbottom went to collect the tractor and trailer, and Mr. Coatsworth went back to the bus, put Mr. and Mrs. Ramsbottom's tandem in it, and drove round to the farm to meet them.

12

'WHAT A SCOOP!'

When Mrs. Ramsbottom saw the dried-up sandwiches (which the birds had had a go at anyway), she
insisted on bringing out a huge ham, cold chicken, a
dish of tomatoes, freshly baked bread, and an enormous slab of farmhouse butter.

'Well!' said Miss Beaver after they'd finished the
delicious apple pie and jug of thick cream that Mrs.
Ramsbottom had brought out for pudding. 'What an
exciting day it turned out to be, just think . . .'

'Excuse me,' a voice interrupted eagerly.

'Goodness!' said Miss Beaver in surprise, as a man's
head popped up from behind a hedge.

'You wouldn't mind if I interviewed you, would
you?' the young man inquired anxiously, his eyes
darting from one child to another.

'Oh, marvellous, marvellous!' he exclaimed, when
Miss Beaver shook her head.

'I'm Old Amos from the *Clarion*,' he added,
leaping agilely over the hedge and nearly tripping
over Avril's coat in his haste to get to them.

'Old Amos and His Country Rambles,' he

explained, looking at Miss Beaver's puzzled face. 'Every Thursday. Approximately two hundred words. Although to be honest,' he added, straightening his tie and flicking a piece of mud off his highly polished shoe with his handkerchief, 'it's not really my line at all. In fact,' he muttered, wrinkling his nose and looking distastefully across the fields, 'I don't even like the country.'

'Old Amos,' Mr. Coatsworth repeated thoughtfully. 'Ah!' he said, slapping his leg. 'I remember now. I read one of your articles once about sheep-clipping.'

'Oh!' said Miss Beaver, as the dapper young man grimaced at the mention of sheep. 'You're a reporter!'

'A reporter!' echoed the children excitedly. 'A reporter. He's come for our story!'

'Actually,' the young man said, frowning, 'I was supposed to be covering the local Hunt, but I can't seem to find it, so I thought I might pepper up the article with an interview with children.' He glanced at Miss Beaver. 'You are from a school, I expect? London?' he inquired eagerly. Miss Beaver nodded again. 'Good,' continued the reporter. 'Well, if you could perhaps give me your views . . .'

'It was like this,' Avril interrupted. 'Miss Beaver left her bag on the bus! . . .'

'Then it got mixed up with the robbers,' Morgan added.

'And when they realized, they dressed up as Mr. and Mrs. Ramsbottom . . .' said Dominic.

248

'And locked the real farmer and his wife in the bedroom,' said Akbar.

'And don't forget the chase,' Jessica chimed in, 'where we nearly crashed lots of times and they'd got teacher on the bus and were threatening her with a gun, and . . .'

'But it was the aniseed balls what did it really,' Avril interrupted as the reporter looked at them blankly, laughed uncertainly, then turned to Miss Beaver.

'Marvellous imagination, children,' he murmured, 'marvellous!'

'But it's absolutely true!' Miss Beaver said in surprise. 'Didn't you know? The children captured the robbers, and in fact,' she added proudly, 'Sergeant Pattison said they would probably be National Heroes by tomorrow!'

'And we're getting a reward too,' Avril finished grandly.

The young man sank to the ground, staring at Miss Beaver in disbelief. 'You mean to say,' he asked weakly, 'that they actually caught two criminals?'

'Yes,' said Miss Beaver firmly.

'And retrieved the money that the robbers had stolen,' Mr. Coatsworth added.

'Oh my!' said the reporter dreamily. 'What a story! What A STORY!!' he repeated, striking his head with his fist and jumping up. 'Children,' he shouted excitedly, 'allow me to introduce myself, Mike Spilligan, special crime reporter! Now, where's my pen?' he muttered, searching feverishly in his pockets. 'Oh,

249

imagine it, imagine it,' he murmured to himself. 'What a scoop. No more nasty sheep, no more foot and mouth, no more footrot, NO MORE OLD AMOS!' he shouted triumphantly, pulling a pen and a notebook from his inside pocket and flourishing them at the bewildered children. And after he'd taken all the details down, he ran to the farmhouse, telephoned his story to every national newspaper and the B.B.C., and when all the children had had a last look at the bull, said good-bye to Mr. and Mrs. Ramsbottom, and climbed onto the coach to go home, he was still dancing round the farmyard ecstatically, murmuring, 'What a scoop, what a scoop!'

13

WELCOME HOME, HEROES

'Well!' Miss Beaver smiled at the children who were going through the events of the day, detail by detail. 'We're nearly home now.'

'And I must say,' proclaimed Mr. Coatsworth, 'it's the best school outing I've ever been on!'

'And me!' said Morgan, Dominic, Jessica, Akbar, and all the rest of the children, thinking about the exciting chase across the fields and the capture of Sid and Bert.

'And they did have a bull after all,' Avril added, sighing contentedly.

'Goodness,' exclaimed Miss Beaver as the bus turned into New End, 'what a lot of noise!'

The children pressed their noses to the bus windows to see what was happening.

'Crikey!' shouted Morgan, looking at the crowd of people outside the school who surged forward, cheering and waving when they saw the bus approaching.

'Look!' cried Dominic. 'Television cameras!'

'And reporters!' shouted Akbar. Photographers jostled each other, taking pictures of the bus.

'Hello, Dad!' Avril screamed, opening the bus window and waving to a figure at the back of the crowd. 'I saw a bull!'

'Oooh!' whispered Jessica, as Mr. Coatsworth stopped the bus to avoid running over the reporters. 'I hope we don't get trampled to death like that cowboy did in the film.'

Miss Beaver had difficulty in opening the doors because of the crowd, and it wasn't until the policemen linked arms and formed a clearing around the bus that she, Mr. Coatsworth, and the children could step down.

The crowd went wild with excitement. The waiting parents were so overcome they had to blow their noses, and the children from the other classes, who had wriggled their way to the front of the crowd to get a better view, started chanting

'2–4–6–8
Who do we appreciate?
C–L–A–S–S
CLASS 6!'

The headmaster, who'd wriggled to the front of the crowd too, clapped his hands together in delight and beamed with pride.

'Goodness,' Miss Beaver murmured, as the Mayor stepped forward to greet them, 'that young man from the *Clarion* certainly spread the news!'

'Welcome home, heroes,' said the Mayor, holding his hand up for silence. 'I would like to take this opportunity to invite you all to a civic reception in your honour, where the Chief Constable of Scotland Yard will present you with the reward.'

'Hooray!' screamed the crowd, stamping their feet in approval.

'And now,' he added, smiling at Miss Beaver, 'perhaps you could tell us personally how you first became involved with the bank robbers.'

'Well,' said Miss Beaver shyly, 'it all started when I mislaid my holdall . . .'

'Let's see it, Miss!' chorused the reporters, who had their cameras poised to take a picture of it.

'Certainly.' Miss Beaver smiled.

And while she climbed into the bus to look for it, the headmaster, who had ducked under the policemen's legs, waved his arms wildly in the air.

'Three cheers for Morgan!' he shouted.

'HIP-HIP-HOORAY!' the crowd screamed.

'Three cheers for Dominic!'

'HIP-HIP-HOORAY!'

'Three cheers for Jessica!'

'HIP-HIP-HOORAY!'

'Three cheers for Akbar!'

'HIP-HIP-HOORAY!'

'Three cheers for Avril!'

'HIP-HIP-HOORAY!!!'

When the headmaster had been through the list of children in Class 6, name by name, and Miss Beaver and Mr. Coatsworth too, and the crowd had roared themselves hoarse, Miss Beaver reappeared.

'Oh dear!' she said to the expectant crowd, laughing awkwardly, 'I'm dreadfully sorry. But – er,' she paused guiltily, 'I seem to have mislaid it!'

ABOUT THE AUTHORS IN THIS BOOK

BARBARA ROBINSON

Barbara Robinson is an American author whose stories about the outrageous Herdman family and their school antics make for some riotous reading. They were published over twenty years ago and have been read and enjoyed by millions of children before you. Perhaps that proves that school life hasn't changed very much!

CHRIS ASHLEY

Chris Ashley is well qualified to write about life in school as he is the headmaster of a primary school in Bury. He began writing for children in 1987 and wrote WASIM IN THE DEEP END as a relaxing break from his school work.

PAT HUTCHINS

Pat Hutchins lives in London and is a prolific children's writer. Her other titles include THE MONA LISA MYSTERY, THE CURSE OF THE EGYPTIAN MUMMY, THE HOUSE THAT SAILED AWAY and RATS! Many of her novels are illustrated by her husband but she is a picture book illustrator in her own right and her famous story for younger readers, ROSIE'S WALK is a classic.

IF YOU HAVE ENJOYED READING THE STORIES IN THIS COLLECTION WHY NOT TRY SOME OF THESE OTHER TITLES BY THE SAME AUTHORS?

Other Red Fox Story Collections

Three in One Ballet Stories
Three in One Animal Stories
Completely Wild Stories